TRUTH AND CONSEQUENCES

LENORA WORTH

HARLEQUIN® LOVE INSPIRED® SUSPENSE

Special thanks and acknowledgment are given to Lenora Worth
for her contribution to the Rookie K-9 Unit miniseries

Recycling programs
for this product may
not exist in your area.

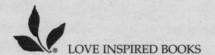

LOVE INSPIRED BOOKS

ISBN-13: 978-0-373-67749-8

Truth and Consequences

"You were amazing out there," David said.

He meant that. "If anything had happened to you—"

Whitney shook her head. "Your overly protective attitude is kind of chivalrous, but I told you I had it covered. I can take care of myself."

"And I told you, I wasn't about to leave you there."

"Would you have left a male officer?" she asked.

David glanced at her, hoping to make her understand. But she had him on that one.

"But because I'm a rookie and a woman, you felt the need to rush in and help me. Don't do that again."

Wow. She sure had a chip on her pretty shoulder. Seemed she also had a lot to prove. "It's not in my nature to just leave a woman alone when she could be in danger. I'm not sorry I stayed."

"Well, cowboy, I do appreciate your assistance, but hopefully there won't be another time for you to play the hero."

ROOKIE K-9 UNIT:
These lawmen solve the toughest cases with the help of their brave canine partners

Lenora Worth writes award-winning romance and romantic suspense. Three of her books finaled in the ACFW Carol Awards, and her Love Inspired Suspense novel *Body of Evidence* became a *New York Times* bestseller. Her novella in *Mistletoe Kisses* made her a *USA TODAY* bestselling author. With sixty books published and millions in print, she goes on adventures with her retired husband, Don, and enjoys reading, baking and shopping...especially shoe shopping. Visit her on the web at lenoraworth.com.

Visit the Author Profile page at Harlequin.com for more titles.

For where envying and contention is,
there is inconstancy, and every evil work.
–James 3:16

Many thanks to my fellow writers in this series—
Terri Reed, Lynette Eason, Shirlee McCoy, Dana Mentink
and Valerie Hansen. I loved working with all of you.

ONE

"Next stop, Desert Valley, Arizona."

David Evans took a deep breath and got up to exit the passenger train, glad to finally be at his destination. Now if he could locate the woman he'd come here to see.

There were only two other people left in this car. Two men wearing baseball caps and dark shades. They'd kept to themselves most of the trip from Los Angeles, and so had David. There was something about these two.

They grabbed their carry-on duffels and rushed out of their seats so fast they stumbled upon the car attendant coming up the aisle. Startled, one of them dropped his tattered black bag, causing it to rip open.

Several colorful bundles covered in shrink-wrap crashed onto the floor. Everything after that happened so fast—David's blood pressure spiked, and he felt himself slipping back into the arid mountains of Afghanistan.

The attendant's surprise turned to realization, his gaze moving from the two men to the packages spilling from the duffel.

"Keep moving, old man," one of the men told the attendant. "Don't you have someplace else to be?"

The attendant stared at the bag. "No, can't do that. I'm afraid I'll have to report this immediately."

"Wrong answer." One of them pulled a knife on the frightened older attendant, stabbing him in the stomach. The attendant went down on his knees, shock and fear evident in his wide-eyed stare.

David saw the whole thing from his seat a few feet up the aisle. While the two argued about leaving without the packages they'd dropped, David hurried to help the injured man.

But one of the men pulled out a gun and pointed it at David, his expression hard-edged while his trigger finger twitched. "Get out of here. Now."

David glanced up at the man holding a gun on him and then down at the bleeding man lying on the floor of the passenger train. "I'm not leaving. I'm a medic, and this man needs help."

He braced himself and knelt down beside the attendant, fully expecting to be shot. Which was kind of ironic since he'd just returned from Afghanistan. He'd managed to survive the front lines, and now he might be killed while trying to honor the promise he'd made to a dying soldier.

Before the standoff could continue, voices outside caused the gunman's friend to whirl in a nervous dance. "I didn't agree to this," he said in a growling whisper, his oversize red baseball cap covering most of his face. "Man, if you shoot him, the DEA and every cop around here will be on us. We need to leave."

The man holding the gun glanced around, the sweat of panic radiating off him like hot steam. Then he spouted off to his short but wise buddy, his words as brittle as desert sand. "Get all that up and let's go. Now!"

He kept the gun on David while his nervous helper shoved the packages back inside the gaping duffel. "You better keep traveling, mister, if you want to live." Then he pointed to the moaning attendant. "I'll finish off both of you if either of you talks."

David held his breath and stayed on his knees near the injured attendant while the two men rushed off the train, baseball caps pulled low over their faces and sunglasses hiding their eyes. But the minute he saw them heading for a black SUV in the small parking lot near the square Tudor-style train station, he pulled out his cell and called 911. Straining to see, he memorized only part of the license plate and quickly glanced at what looked like some sort of Aztec emblem centered over the plates.

"I'm a medic," he told the shocked older man after giving the dispatcher the needed information. "I'm going to help you, okay?" He checked the man's vitals and found a weak pulse.

The pale-faced man nodded, his expression full of fright, his pupils dilating as he went into shock. "He stabbed me."

"I saw," David said. Taking off the button-up shirt over his old T-shirt, he quickly used it to stanch the blood oozing from the gash in the man's abdomen. "Lie still while I examine you. Help should be on the way."

The man moaned and closed his eyes. "My wife is gonna be so mad."

David sank down beside the man, hoping to keep him talking. "Hey, buddy, what's your name?"

"Herman," the man said. "Herman Gallagher." Then he grabbed David's arm. "You need to report this to our conductor, too. Drugs. I think they had drugs in those bags."

David did as he asked, and soon the conductor and several attendants were moving up and down the aisles.

David put up a hand to hold them away and

kept talking to the man after handing his phone to a young assistant, who stayed on the line with 911. When he heard sirens, he breathed a sigh of relief. Though he was concerned because of Mr. Gallagher's age and still disoriented himself, he'd seen much worse than this in the heat of battle. But right now, he was struggling to fight his own flashbacks.

This trip had sure ended with a bang.

And he hadn't even stepped off the train to his final destination.

He'd come here searching for a woman he didn't really know, except in his imagination. But a promise was a promise. He wasn't leaving Desert Valley without finding her.

When he looked up a few minutes later to see a pretty female officer with long blond hair coming toward him, a sleek tan-and-white canine pulling on a leash in front of her, David thought he surely must be dreaming. Either that or his flashbacks were taking a new turn.

He knew that face. Had seen it in his dreams many times over.

While he sat on the cold train floor holding a bloody shirt to a man who was about to pass out, he looked up and into the vivid blue eyes of the woman he'd traveled here to find. The woman who'd colored his dreams during the brutality of war and made him wish he could finally settle down. Thinking of the worn picture in his pocket that her brother, Lucas, had given him right before he died, David couldn't believe this was really happening.

Whitney Godwin was coming to his aid.

Whitney took one look at the two men on the train floor and went into action. Turning to her partner, a white-and-tan pointer appropriately named Hunter, she commanded, "Stay."

Hunter whimpered, his shiny nose sniffing the air, his dark eyes lifting to her in a definite alert. Did the big dog sense something else around here? Hunter was trained in drug detection, so it was possible. They'd both recently finished an intense twelve-week session in town, so Whitney knew they were up to the task. Yet her heart beat with a burst of adrenaline that shouted, *This is the real deal*.

She took a good look at the injured train attendant and the man helping him. They'd both have to be questioned and cleared. "We'll get to our search later, Hunter."

Turning from Hunter, she spoke into the radio attached to her shoulder. "James, need that bus, stat. We have one injured and one who doesn't look so hot." Then she added, "We need to clear the train, too. Hunter's a little antsy."

"Bus is en route. ETA three minutes," James

Harrison, fellow rookie, responded. "I'll take Hawk and have a look around, question some of the bystanders. Ellen's on the way. She and Carly can help with a sweep."

Ellen Foxcroft was also a rookie, and her golden retriever, Carly, was trained in tracking. Her mother, the formidable Marian Foxcroft, who'd always been supportive of the K9 training program in Desert Valley, had recently made an offer to Chief Jones that he couldn't ignore. They'd all been asked to stay here after graduation from the training course to help investigate the high-profile murder of their master trainer, Veronica Earnshaw.

Marian had offered to underwrite their salaries since she wanted Veronica's murder solved right away. Not to mention, she wanted the two suspicious deaths of two former rookies to be declared accidents once and for all. Marian didn't like any black marks on the Desert Valley Police Department's record. But someone seemed to have a beef with Marian, too, since she'd been found unconscious in her home a few weeks ago and was still in a coma at the Canyon County Regional Medical Center located twenty miles west of Desert Valley. Ellen had requested round-the-clock security for her mother's room. They were all on high alert.

"Roger that," Whitney responded to James.

While the rookies were still in Desert Valley, they took whatever calls they could to gain experience. James's dog, Hawk, a bloodhound trained in crime scene investigations, would sniff out any evidence. And she'd get Hunter on that, too. "I'll stay with the eyewitness."

Then she turned to the railroad employees and urged them to keep away the anxious passengers craning their necks to see what had happened. Her fellow officers would conduct interviews with the few passengers waiting to return to the train. Maybe they, or some of the passengers about to board for the first time, had seen something.

Whitney leaned over the two men. "Hey, I'm Officer Whitney Godwin with the Desert Valley K9 Unit." *For now.* Just until she could get through this murder investigation and, she hoped, move back to Tucson. Centering her gaze on the young, good-looking one, she asked, "Can you tell me what happened here?"

He nodded and blinked as if refocusing, his hand splayed across a bloody shirt covering the other man's wound. "Two men came up the aisle, heading for the exit." He pointed to his left, indicating the third coach seat from the door. "They had two big duffels, and they ran smack into Mr. Gallagher here." He stopped and sucked in a breath. "A bag ripped open and packages fell everywhere. All different colors but about the same size. Pretty obvious that they were carrying drugs."

Whitney nodded and took notes. No wonder Hunter was champing at the bit. Drugs? "Okay. What happened after that?"

"One of them stabbed Mr. Gallagher." He motioned to the injured man. "That same one saw me moving up the aisle and pulled a gun on me, but when they heard voices outside, the other man talked him out of shooting me. They grabbed their duffels and left. I watched them get into a dark SUV in the parking lot."

He checked the injured man's pulse and talked to him in soothing, reassuring tones. "Hang on, Mr. Gallagher. Help is coming."

Whitney went over her notes to make sure she had everything, his soothing voice calming her, too. He had a distinctive accent, a Southern drawl. "Did they pull a gun on the victim?"

"No. He surprised them. The man stabbed him, probably to keep anyone from hearing. But I saw the whole thing, so he pulled the gun on me." David shook his head. "I guess they thought everyone had exited already, and we both surprised them."

"He's telling the truth," Mr. Gallagher said in a weak voice. "He threatened this young man if he talked. Threatened me, too, but I'm not scared of any criminal. Drug runners are getting mighty bold these days."

"Got it," Whitney said, glancing at the man aiding the victim. Obviously he hadn't taken that threat seriously, either. "And again, where were you, sir, when this took place?"

He looked up at her with deep brown eyes that were now clear and sure. "The last seat on the right, near the door to the next car. I... I'm an army medic. I mean, I'm a former army medic."

"Army medic?" That brought a heavy pain to Whitney's heart. Her brother had been a sergeant in the army. But he'd been killed almost a year ago. Before she could figure out how to tell him about all the changes in her life.

I made it, Lucas. She had so much she wanted to tell her big brother, such as that she'd passed through her second stint of training without a hitch and that she had an amazing responsibility in her life, her baby daughter, Shelby, but now it was too late.

At least her brother had accepted her choice of careers before he'd died. Wishing he could have seen her graduate after her second attempt to finish the rigorous twelve-week K9 training here in Desert Valley, Whitney pushed aside the too-sad thoughts of her brother and got back to her job.

"Okay, that's good. You're both doing great. The paramedics should be here any minute."

Already she could hear another dog barking. Probably one of her fellow rookies coming to help out. They were all stuck here on the big investigation into the murder of Veronica Earnshaw and the suspicious deaths of the two rookies.

Whitney didn't have time right now to think about those deaths, even though she'd been personally involved with one of the victims.

For now this stabbing had to be her top priority. She needed to get the details right or she'd hear an earful from Chief Jones. The chief had her on his radar since she'd gone to him with a theory regarding one of those deaths, a theory he'd found hard to believe. If she messed this up, he might think she wasn't qualified for the job.

The medic seemed calmer now, so she hoped she could trust his eyewitness details to be accurate. He seemed capable and sure, even if he was a bit disoriented.

Then, because she wanted to know, and needed to know for her report, she asked, "What's your name?"

"David Evans." He waited as if he expected her to say something else, his brown eyes bright with anticipation.

Whitney wrote his name in her notes. They'd

run a background check on him. "You're passing through?"

With what looked like relief in his eyes, he shook his head. "No. I'm here to stay for a while. Maybe."

Surprised, Whitney added that to her notes. "Welcome to Desert Valley."

He gave her a tight smile. "Thanks. Is it always like this?"

Whitney shook her head. "No. More like routine traffic stops and bar brawls. But…we do get some drug runners through here now and then." She glanced back at her anxious partner. Hunter wanted to get on the move. "Did you happen to see the license plate on the SUV?"

He squinted, blinked. "I…I think. But only partly. The numbers one and five and…and several letters that might be some sort of vanity plate. I can't remember the name, but there was a symbol over the plate—on the back of the SUV. I didn't get the details, but it was small. I got a quick glance."

"Maybe it'll come back to you," Whitney said, observing his clipped chestnut-brown hair. He seemed to be in good shape other than the shock that must have hit him right after he'd witnessed all of this. But he wore a mantle of weariness, too. He looked world-weary and rugged, almost haggard. And tired.

She jotted down what he'd said. "Can you describe the two men?"

"I'm not sure of their race, but both had dark hair, and they were kind of disguised and wearing baseball caps—one was red. The guy who stabbed Mr. Gallagher and pointed a gun at me—he had a thick beard and longer hair, and he wore a black hat. He was tall. The other one was shorter. They had on sunglasses." He gave her their estimated heights and weights. "And… they both had the same kind of dark bag. Old and worn and full of what looked like birthday gifts or some kind of shipment, but it had to be drugs."

"We'll do a thorough check of the train," she said, never doubting he was correct. Mr. Gallagher was right. This was happening a lot lately.

When Whitney heard sirens, she breathed easier. The heat inside the train was stifling even though it was early spring. She wouldn't go home until she and Hunter had sniffed and searched this entire train and talked to the other employees and questioned the few passengers who waited to board. She was relieved that help for this injured man was on the way.

"You did a good job," she told David. "Now you can relax and let my friends take over."

But Mr. Brown Eyes grabbed her arm. "I'm

pretty sure those two will try something else. Drug couriers are ruthless, pretty packages aside."

Whitney nodded, suspecting the same thing. "My partner, Hunter, will alert if any drugs have been transported, and we'll put out a BOLO on the suspects."

When they heard the paramedics coming onto the train, David turned to Mr. Gallagher. "The posse's here, sir. You'll be in good hands. I know you're in pain, but I think you'll be fine. The wound isn't as deep as it feels and thankfully, from what I can tell, the knife didn't hit any major organs." He glanced at Whitney. "I'll give them the rundown on his vitals."

"Thank you, son," the older man said. "You're a hero."

"You're welcome, sir," David replied, wearing an embarrassed expression, his face coloring.

Mr. Gallagher nodded. "And thank you for serving our country."

David's eyes met Whitney's, a pain etched there in the dark irises. "Yes, sir."

Whitney got the feeling that he wanted to say something else. Maybe the newcomer knew more about all of this than he was willing to divulge right now.

TWO

David leaned against the back of the old Crown Victoria and waited for Officer Godwin and her K9 partner, Hunter, to return. The ambulance had left, and two other patrol cars were now leaving. The impatient passengers who wanted to continue their journeys were waiting inside the quaint little train station while the K9 officers inspected their luggage piled up outside. As far as he knew, none of them had witnessed the event or the two men leaving the train. Suitcase by suitcase, their luggage was cleared so they could board.

Maybe he should do that, too. He could keep drifting, forget his troubles and…try to find a normal life again.

But he wasn't about to go anywhere until he knew Whitney was safe. Which was stupid, really. She was the one with a gun and a trained canine partner. She could certainly take care of herself, based on what Lucas had told him and based on what he'd seen here today. She might look like a cheerleader, but she was all business on the job.

According to Lucas, Whitney was stubborn and hugely independent. When they'd first met, Lucas had proudly explained that after a couple of years as a beat cop back in Tucson, Whitney had been accepted as part of a training program for K9 officers based here in Desert Valley. But he'd had concerns about the whole thing since he knew the work could be grueling and dangerous. They'd argued before he deployed, but after admitting that no one had stopped *him* from following his own path, Lucas had finally emailed Whitney and apologized, only to learn that she'd had to drop out of the program. David had no doubt that Lucas loved his sister.

"She had some trouble, but she's gonna try again next spring," Lucas had stated a few days before he'd been wounded. "That's Whitney. She never gives up."

Lucas had died a week later. That had been last summer.

It had taken David months to get here. After finishing his deployment and returning stateside, he'd fought against this quest. He hadn't even been home to Texas yet, mainly because there wasn't much left there for him. Now that he was here, he was pretty sure Whitney would be shocked and surprised that he'd followed through on a deathbed promise to her brother.

And yet he couldn't leave her. He kept watching the shadows of her long ponytail, the silhouette of her moving through the train for one last search. He'd watched in amazement earlier as the sleek, powerful dog—a pointer, she'd told him—did just that, pointed near the seats where those two men had been. Hunter had stopped with his nose in the air, his tail lifted in statuelike stillness. Then he'd become agitated and aggressive, growling low while he pawed the floor by the seats.

After Whitney had encouraged Hunter to "Go find," the big dog had sniffed and pawed. They'd found a package wrapped to look like a gift box that had slid under the seat when the bag had torn open. Obviously the two couriers hadn't seen it when they'd dropped part of the duffel's contents. But the lone package they'd left behind would create a lot more than birthday-party memories. Heroin. With a street value of hundreds of thousands of dollars per kilo, according to what he'd heard Whitney and some of the others discussing.

Hunter sniffed out a couple more spots, two sleeping car closets and two bathrooms. David heard Whitney telling one of the officers that drugs had obviously been transported in those areas, too, since he'd alerted on both.

"No telling how long they've been using this route," she'd said to an older, distinguished-looking man she'd addressed as Chief Jones. "We'll have to study the video cameras and the passenger manifest, too. Maybe pick up an image or establish a pattern."

Now David looked up to find her walking toward him with another K9 officer she'd introduced as Ellen Foxcroft, a native of Desert Valley, and her K9 partner, Carly, a golden retriever specializing in tracking.

"Thanks," Whitney said to her friend after they stopped by Ellen's vehicle. "So we know based on Carly's alert and Hawk's detection of that dusty shoe print that they got into a vehicle here in the lot, as our witness reported."

Ellen listened to Whitney and then glanced over at David and nodded. "And based on the partial plate your witness here was able to remember, we might be able to find that vehicle soon." She nodded to David and then opened the door to her vehicle to let Carly inside the back. "I'll talk to you tomorrow, Whitney. We'll compare notes."

Whitney agreed and then turned to give David a dark scowl, her blue eyes flashing aggravation. Aside from the frown on her pretty face, she looked kind of cute in her uniform. She was buff but she was also dainty, like a fragile flower. Only she was way too fierce to be a flower. One tough female. David's heart beat an extra thump at the danger she had to put herself through in order to do her job.

Same as her brother.

"Why are you still here?" she asked, suspicion lacing the question. "We've cleared the scene, and I have to file an official report. I have your contact information. You're free to go until we call you in to look at mug shots."

"I'm waiting on you," he said, thinking if he told her he'd stayed behind to keep an eye on her, she'd laugh in his face. David didn't think right now would be a good time to explain that her late brother had sent him here.

"You really don't need to worry about me," she retorted. Glancing back at the train and then at her alert partner, she said, "We didn't find anything else during that last sweep. But we dusted for prints on the seats where we found the one package, and we found some shoe prints, so maybe those clues will turn something up."

David waited while she gave Hunter water and food from two tin buckets she had clipped inside his wire kennel in her police car.

"You did a good job, Hunter," she mumbled

in a sweet voice that tickled at David's senses like butterfly wings. "Such a good boy."

Hunter gave her a grateful stare and started gnawing on a rope throw that David guessed was his chew treat after each find. David gave her an appraising glance and realized how tough she was underneath that porcelain doll skin and sunshine-blond hair.

Satisfied, she turned to David. "Where are you headed?"

"I don't know, honestly. I'm on some R & R right now, meandering around the West, taking in the sights. Maybe volunteering to help here and there. Thought I'd find a place nearby for the night."

So I can stay near you for a while.

Her suspicions hit like sunspots all around him. "There's a bed-and-breakfast in town. The Desert Rose, right off Desert Valley Drive. You might find a room there. Just until you decide which way you want to go."

Then she gave him a no-nonsense stare. "Of course, you need to stick around anyway in case you can help us identify those two. I'll talk to the chief and see if we need to call you in to the station tomorrow."

He nodded, taking advantage of the intro. "Why not now? I can go to the station tonight since I'm in no hurry."

She checked her watch. "We've put out a bulletin on any dark SUVs matching your description, but drug couriers are notorious for switching up vehicles or changing license plates. Look, it's late, and I have to be somewhere. First thing tomorrow, okay? But if you remember anything before then, here's my card."

In spite of everything that had happened, David was almost glad he had a legitimate excuse to stay in town. He pocketed her business card, also grateful for the contact number.

"I did some searches online when I decided to take this trip. I found some information about the Desert Valley Clinic. One article mentioned the need for more funding and more doctors. They use volunteer doctors, physician's assistants, and nurses for the free services they offer." He'd have to sign a waiver to get a temporary license to practice at free clinics in the state. "Thought I might volunteer there while I'm here. Don't want to get rusty."

"And exactly why are you *here* when you could be anywhere in the world right now?" she asked, her eyes scanning the train again before she whipped her gaze back to him. "Because I've never heard of anyone wanting to spend downtime in Desert Valley or wanting to *volunteer* to work with Dr. Pennington."

David braced himself and stored up her

pointed notations for future reference. He'd have to be careful with this one. Whitney would keep digging until she had him figured out. "Well—"

But Whitney Godwin was no longer listening to him. She held up her finger and then, giving Hunter a silent command, drew her weapon and took off in a crouched run toward the empty train.

A man scurried toward the train like a lizard, his head down and his back hunched. He wore a burgundy hat and dark shades.

Whitney spotted him when she glanced back while talking with David. She'd have to figure out the medic's angle and his story later. Right now, she intended to nab two criminals. With her gun drawn and Hunter waiting for her command as he trailed along, she hurried around the stopped train and looked up and down the tracks.

Nothing. No one. Had she only imagined seeing someone? No, she'd seen the man, and his description had fit the one David Evans and Mr. Gallagher had given her. She hadn't slept much last night, but she wasn't imagining things. Fatigue weighed on her like a blanket of dry heat, but she kept her cool and went on with doing her job. Being a rookie meant she always had to go the extra mile. Being a female police officer meant she had to work twice as hard as the men around her.

She checked the front of the stopped train again and then walked by the narrow openings between the four small passenger cars, and headed to the car where she and Hunter had found a kilo of heroin earlier.

"C'mon, Hunter," she commanded. Hunter went in ahead of her, doing his job with practiced excitement. He sniffed and moved on, sniffed again, dug around some and then kept up the search.

Could one of these men have come back for the package they'd dropped? Or did they have more stashed elsewhere?

Thinking it was mighty bold of this one to creep back so soon after they'd taken off earlier, Whitney glanced around. They'd allowed the few passengers traveling west to get back on, but some of the passenger cars were still empty.

Easy for someone to slip in and hide.

Whitney moved behind Hunter up the aisle, careful to search every compartment and seat. When they didn't find anything, she shook her head and wiped at the sweat dripping down her brow. It would be so nice to get home and have a long shower. But she had reports to file and other obligations to consider.

And one very good-looking medic hanging

around for no good reason. Her suspicions regarding David Evans increased by the minute. His excuse for being here didn't make sense to her practical way of thinking. And yet he'd put his own life on the line to help the injured attendant, and he'd cooperated fully with the police. He'd answered her questions without hesitation.

Maybe she was too tired to have any clear thoughts right now.

"Let's get out of here," she said to Hunter, her gut telling her the criminal was still lurking somewhere near the train.

They exited the train and she did one last sweep, checking between the sleek cars, looking underneath, turning toward the scraggly woods.

Then Hunter let out a guttural growl and stood staring at a spot at the end of the train.

"Go ahead," Whitney commanded as she drew her gun and hurried down the side of the tracks near a copse of ponderosa pines, dry shrubs and chaparrals. A few spring wildflowers peeked out in bright orange and red, interspersed underneath a scraggly cactus bush, but she was interested only in seeing what Hunter wanted her to see.

Hunter took off, silent but steady, toward the scattered rocks and shrubs.

Whitney followed. When Hunter alerted again, she crouched down near a jutting rock.

Too late to call for backup. She'd have to do this on her own. Bracing for action, she whirled out from the rock with her weapon ready only to find a dirty black shirt lying on the ground.

Then Hunter started barking. She heard a click behind her. "Halt the dog and drop the gun."

Whitney did as he asked. "Stay," she said to Hunter in a commanding voice, her insides like jelly. Then she slowly laid her gun on the ground, her mind racing. This could go wrong if she lost her cool. Hunter growled low, but he wouldn't attack without her order.

Could she do this? Could she risk having her K9 partner shot in midair? Hunter was still in training, too. What if he got hurt because of her carelessness?

"Stay," she told him again, her tone firm in spite of her trembling nerves.

She glanced back and found a handgun pointed at her head by a tall bearded man wearing a black baseball cap and dark shades. But this wasn't the man she'd seen running beside the train. That man had been wearing the dark red baseball cap and had shorter hair. Which meant he was probably moving through the train car, looking for any lost packages of heroin. They'd set a trap.

"What do you want?" she asked the man who held his gun pointed at her.

"Keep telling the dog to heel," he whispered in a rasp that burned her neck.

Hunter stood growling, ready to attack.

"Stay," Whitney commanded, her pulse pumping adrenaline through her body. "Stay."

Hunter didn't move, but the big dog's whole body shook with aggression, his bared teeth visible.

"One move from you, lady, and that dog and you both die." He twisted her around and jerked her arm with a brutal grasp, his rancid breath hissing against her ear.

"I'm not a lady," she retorted. "I'm a police officer."

The stench of his sweat assaulted her. Sweat and fear. "And a nosy one," he replied on a huff of air. "Shoulda kept going."

He pushed her deeper into the sparse, dry landscape, kicking up dust that made her want to cough. Whitney glanced around, her breath settling. No one had noticed them on the far side of the big train car, and now the train would soon be leaving the station. She wouldn't let this criminal get to her, but she wasn't going to die here, either. She'd get out of this. Somehow.

She'd acted too hastily and made a rookie mistake. She hadn't been careful, and she hadn't called for backup. Hunter would do her bidding, but she had to find the right moment. She'd like to blame her lack of attention to detail on the mysterious medic who'd appeared here and stayed with her. But Whitney wasn't one for pushing off blame on others. This was her mistake.

The man kicked her gun behind him, then shoved her into a cluster of pines and rock. Praying that someone would see what was happening, Whitney kept thinking ahead. He could be bringing her out here for only one reason.

Trying to memorize all the details around her, she took a deep breath. Black Hat had a tattoo on his lower arm. Some sort of intricate symbol. An arrow and three hanging feathers with what looked like a face in the arrow. Could it be the same symbol David Evans had mentioned seeing over the license plate of the SUV?

"So what's your plan?" she asked in a matter-of-fact tone that belied the tremors running through her body. "Where's your buddy?"

"Shut up so I can think," he said into her ear. "We got surprised today, so I have to clean up this mess before the boss finds out."

"Who's your boss? If you agree to cooperate, we might be able to help you out. Think about it. Your boss won't help you."

His voice shook. "Right. I'm not buying that, so shut up."

Whitney could take advantage of his nervous energy.

She prayed for calm and clarity. She'd been one of the best in her class when she'd returned to training this year, so she centered her thoughts on what she'd been taught. Determined to stay alive, she concentrated on her sweet five-month-old baby girl, Shelby. The baby she'd fought so hard to have. Alone. The baby her brother had never heard about because he'd died before she'd found the courage to tell him.

Whitney would regret for the rest of her life that Lucas would never know his niece. But she would fight for her child's sake, too.

She was at her best when she was cornered and alone.

The man shoved her toward the tumbleweeds and scrub brush that surrounded the scant trees and jutting rocks. "Let's get this done and over."

The train now hissed like a big snake. He was waiting for the train to leave. It would serve as a cover when he shot her. So that meant his friend must have made it off the train without detection.

Adrenaline pumped a new energy through Whitney's system. She had to act fast or she'd never see Shelby again.

She went limp so she could use her body to get away from the man holding her. It worked. Her body fell against the man, causing his hands to go up and giving her enough time to slip a booted foot behind his left calf and bring him down. But on the way down, she heard a grunt and then felt a blur of air rushing by her head. The next thing she knew, the man who'd been holding her let out a yelp of pain and dropped at her feet, his gun sliding over dry dirt and skidding to a stop a few feet away.

Surprised, she watched in amazement as a now familiar form crashed over the gunman who'd been about to shoot her and held him pinned to the ground.

THREE

The medic! She'd forgotten all about him. With a grunt, he lifted his right arm and hit the man on the head with a big jagged rock. Which didn't do much in the way of injuries, so it wouldn't keep him down long. But it gave David time to get up and Whitney enough time to react. Flipping the man over, she motioned to David, and he helped her control the man on the ground.

Hunter growled and danced, eyeing her for instructions.

"Guard," Whitney ordered as she scrambled up, her breath leaving her body. David helped her, steadying her until she caught her breath and searched for her radio. The dog stood over the moaning man.

"He'll bite you if I tell him to," Whitney informed the man. "It's up to you, but I strongly suggest you stay still and remain on your stomach."

David glanced around and then spotted her

gun. He grabbed it and held it on the man, who was now curled up with Hunter hovering over him. "Are you okay?" he asked Whitney.

She nodded and then reached out to David. "Give me the gun."

David looked uncertain and then shook his head. "I'd feel better if you get him cuffed."

Whitney debated and then nodded while she leaned over the suspect. "Now it's your turn to stay still, or I will let my partner here tear you to shreds."

Panic poured off the criminal on the ground. His eyes widened in fear, his gaze darting here and there. "*My* partner will be here soon."

"No, he won't," David said. "I saw him heading the other way about five minutes ago. He left you."

And the train was finally leaving the station. Once it was well up the tracks in a fading echo, the desert went quiet. Whitney reached for her cuffs, using her strength to hold the man while she tried to slap the restraints against his wrists.

But the man on the ground turned desperate. He rolled and came at her with both feet kicking, causing her to flip in the air before she ever got the first cuff secured. Hunter barked and danced while Whitney felt herself sliding on dry rock, her knees and hands burning with heat and friction, the cuffs slipping out of her grip. The criminal and she both reached and grabbed for the handgun he'd lost before, the weapon out of reach between them. Hunter went into frenzied barking while Whitney fought with a person who had twice her strength.

David grabbed the man and lifted him away before the criminal could get to the gun. This time, David put a booted foot on the man's chest and held her gun to the man's head.

"Don't even think about it," David said, his tone deep and full of rage. "I'll shoot you in the leg and damage you for life. If you doubt me, I can show you which artery I'll hit. You might bleed to death before help can come."

The man spewed out a round of nasty words, but Whitney saw him eyeing David as if he didn't believe him. She hustled into action, grabbed her lost radio and took her gun back from David.

She motioned to the man. "On your stomach again."

This criminal would not give in. He gave both of them a quick glance and then stared at Hunter before he jumped up, knocked her down again and then sprinted across the rocks with all his might. David threw his body over hers, holding her gun aimed at the man who was now running toward the open tracks.

Pain shooting up her arms, she commanded

Hunter to "Bite," and then watched the man getting away, Hunter chasing him.

A black SUV slid up next to the tracks, its tires burning rubber and slinging dirt and rocks. The driver opened the passenger-side door. "Hurry. We'll take care of this later."

The man sped up, but Hunter nipped at his pants and tore part of the left pants leg away before the suspect threw himself inside the vehicle. It took off while he was still climbing inside. Hunter stood with the torn piece of fabric at his feet.

"Hunter, stay!" Whitney screamed at David, "Let me up!"

He rolled away, his gaze following the disappearing SUV.

"Give me my gun!" Whitney lifted herself up and started after them.

But a strong hand grabbed her and tugged her back.

David shook his head. "Let's get out of here," he said into her ear. "It's too dangerous."

"No," she said, disbelief making her angry. "I have to go after them. It's my job, and you're hindering me from doing it."

He held her there, his eyes as rich as dark leather. "They'll kill you."

If he thought that would hold her back, he was mistaken. Whitney pushed up again. Every muscle in her body hurt, and her skin burned with abrasions. "I said, let me go. Now!"

Hunter sensed she might be in danger and growled, his black eyes centered on David.

"I don't like this," she said. "Hunter's reacting to my stress. He thinks you're hurting me."

But David wasn't listening. He glared across the train tracks, watching, waiting, his hand holding her arm. "They've stopped. They might be coming back. They'll ambush you again."

Whitney took in a deep breath and called Hunter to come. She didn't want to agree with the man, but she'd already messed up on so many levels. She couldn't do this alone. Pushing back anger and frustration, she glared at him.

"I have to report in," she said, reaching for her radio as she sank against a rock. After giving the dispatcher her location and a description of the men and the vehicle, she shifted away from David, her body still shaky. "We'll up the search and the BOLO alert."

When she tried to stand, one of her legs buckled. David tucked her weapon into his waistband and then scooped her up into his arms and started walking.

"Put me down," Whitney shouted as David carried her through the heavy brush next to the train tracks. He might be tall and lanky, but the man had surprising strength. She should turn her weapon on *him*.

But when they heard a vehicle's engine revving up down the tracks, Whitney looked up and into David's eyes.

"They're back," he said. "We need to hide and wait for help."

Taking her to a small copse of spindly pines, he gestured to a huge jagged rock, and they crouched behind it, David in front of her as if he were waiting for a battle to begin.

And maybe a battle *was* about to begin. These men were desperate and dangerous.

Whitney glared at him, her breath coming in huffs. "You should have stayed out of this. They know you. They've seen your face. That's why they turned around. They have to eliminate any witnesses."

He inhaled and stared through the bushes. "Yes, they saw my face when they came close to shooting me the first time. I'm trying to keep you from going after them because they know you now, too."

Whitney struggled to find footing, his words sobering. "I don't need your help. I mean it. Let me go."

When they heard hurried footsteps, they stopped arguing.

David glanced at her, relieved. "That's probably one of your patrol officers coming to check on us." Then he gave her an imploring stare. "You heard those men. They'll keep coming. To deal with this problem."

Whitney had the distinct feeling that he wasn't referring to the other bags of heroin.

"You shouldn't have interfered."

David glanced over at the woman who'd practically forced him to get into her vehicle earlier so she could take him in to give a statement and look at mug shots. After she'd been confronted by the same two men a second time, both Whitney and Chief Jones had decided now would be a good time to identify them.

After they'd both been checked over by the EMTs at the scene and she'd gone over the details with Chief Jones and handed over the suspect's handgun and the torn fabric from his pants as evidence, David had been questioned. Then she'd brought him to the police station, where it seemed the whole rookie team had gathered for some sort of briefing.

David had noticed at least five other K9 officers, four men and one other woman, plus several older officers milling around. For a small-town department, Desert Valley sure had a lot of willing law enforcement personnel right now.

And they'd all checked him out in one way or another.

He'd glanced at mug shots for what seemed like hours. He'd also described what he'd remembered about the symbol he'd seen on the license plate of the SUV. "It looked like an arrow, pointing up. And feathers. Three or four, maybe, dangling down." There was something else, but he couldn't remember what he was missing.

"We get a lot of that around here," Whitney's fellow officer, Eddie Harmon, had said with a shrug. "And we don't have an artist on site to sketch it out for us."

"I saw a tattoo on one of the men's arms," Whitney had told David and Eddie. "Could be the same." She'd glanced over at a tall female officer with short brown hair who had an Amazonian-type build. "Louise, maybe you can do some research on tattoos for us, based on the description."

"I'll see what I can find," the woman had replied.

David had gone back to searching the mug shots, but he was glad Whitney had verified what he'd seen. Maybe it was some sort of cartel symbol or a popular Southwestern tattoo.

But he couldn't match any of the faces in the books to the two men who'd caused all the trouble on the train. Now he wondered if they'd both disguised themselves.

"Go home, Godwin," the chief, a tall man with a paunch and thick gray hair, had finally commanded. "And stay home and rest tomorrow morning. You look a little beat up, and I noticed you've been favoring that left leg."

Whitney had frowned, but she hadn't argued with the man. Instead, she'd made a couple of phone calls and seemed anxious to leave the station.

After the two hours or so they'd spent together, she'd also offered to give David a ride to the nearest inn. "It's on the way," she'd explained. "So get in and don't argue with me."

Now back in the squad car with her, and refusing to apologize for coming to her aid, David said, "I was trying to help. There were two of them, and they're obviously ruthless. They might have killed you if I'd left you there."

"But I'm a trained officer," Whitney replied, her blue eyes popping fire. "I could have handled it."

"You're also a rookie," David said. "And Desert Valley isn't exactly a large town."

She stopped the car in front of the Desert Rose B and B, which seemed to live up to its name. The big Victorian house was painted a blush pink and surrounded by rosebushes. "How did you know I was a rookie?"

David realized he'd made a mistake. But he'd learned to listen and observe during his years on the front lines. "I...uh...heard you talking back at the train station, to that other officer—Eddie. I think he was teasing you about it."

Which was true. David had witnessed how the older officer's teasing seemed to rub her the wrong way. To change the subject, he said, "Let me have a look at your hands again."

"My hands are fine," she said, her expression full of fatigue.

"Let me check," he said, his gaze moving over her.

She reluctantly held out her hands.

"You should have let the paramedic bandage these scratches." He reached for her, taking her right hand in his so he could turn it over and look at her palm. In spite of being tough, she had delicate, graceful hands. "Hard to see your wounds in this light, but you need to wash these scratches and cuts with soap and water and make sure you flush all the embedded dirt and rock out. And if you don't have some antibacterial ointment, you need to stop and get some."

"Okay." She pulled her hand away, wincing. "Okay, I'll take care of it. I have soap and I have ointment."

"And stay off that ankle. It might be a light sprain. You need to—"

"RICE," she interrupted, impatient with him. "Rest, ice, compression and elevation. I know the drill, Doc."

David tried to get her to open up. "I guess you're used to slamming bad guys against the rocks, huh?"

"Not really," she admitted. "Only in training up to now. But I got in a lot of quality experience today, I guess."

"You were amazing." He meant that. He was still in awe of her.

Her suspicious stare mellowed to a confused scowl. "Eddie Harmon—the officer you heard teasing me earlier—is totally harmless and probably doesn't even realize he's insulting me. He likes to pick on me since I'm one of the few female officers around here. And he's not much help with an investigation. He's been on the force for thirty years, and I think he's not really into chasing anyone or solving anything. He hates even issuing tickets."

Glad he'd distracted her, David nodded. That older officer was a fine one to talk. "Explains why he left the scene before the rest of you did. If anything had happened to you—"

She shook her head and gave him an aggravated glare. "He likes to get home in time to have dinner with his wife and kids. Your overly protective attitude is kind of chivalrous but I told you, I had it covered."

"And I told you, I wasn't about to leave you there."

"Would you have left a male officer?"

David glanced at her, hoping to make her understand. But she had him on that one. "Okay, probably yes." Then he shrugged. "But I would have called 911 regardless."

"But because I'm a rookie and a woman, you felt the need to rush in and help me. Don't do that again."

Wow. She sure had a chip on her shoulder. Seemed she also had a lot to prove.

"It's not in my nature to leave a woman alone when she could be in danger. I'm not sorry I stayed."

"Well, cowboy, I do appreciate your assistance, but ideally, there won't be another time for you to play the hero."

"I didn't do it to be a hero." David didn't normally get this involved in trying to defend himself. But normally, he could at least form a complete sentence. "Look, I arrived here still reeling from what I'd been through over in Afghanistan. I saw all of this happening in front of my eyes, and I was concerned. Drug runners don't mess around."

She still wasn't happy with him. With a dark frown, she stopped the squad car near the curb and motioned to the Desert Rose. "Go in and get yourself a room. I might need to question you again when I go back over my report, but right now I have to go."

She glanced to Hunter behind a wired screen in the backseat, habitually checking on her partner. "At least we got a good look at their faces." Giving him another serious stare, she added, "I'll be in touch. Take care."

"You take care, too." David saw a flicker of concern pass through her eyes. "Look, if you're worried about those guys—"

"I'm not." Another blue-eyed glare. "I'd like to haul them in, but to do that, I have to go back over everything, including your part in this."

Did she think he *was* part of this? Surely not.

Her next words confirmed that she didn't. "If they see you hanging around, you'll be on their radar. So be careful."

"Same to you. They saw you. Up close." He couldn't stop thinking about that. "What if they come after you?"

"Hunter lives with me. He'll alert."

"And you feel comfortable with that?"

"Yes, I do." She sighed and brushed at the hair escaping her ponytail. "Look, I appreciate your warnings, but...this is my job. I've trained for this, and I worked hard to become a K9 officer. I'll be okay. You watch *your* back, all right?"

"Always." He got out but turned and leaned back into the vehicle. She obviously wasn't ready to listen to reason. And in spite of his misgivings, he wasn't quite ready to blurt out the truth to her. "Thanks for your help today. I'm sorry I overstepped my bounds."

"Relax," she said. "You just got back from what had to be a lot of trauma. It's natural you'd overreact." Then her expression softened. "You remind me of my brother. He was always protective of me."

David's heart did a little lurch. He wanted to tell her that he'd known her brother. But not yet. Not after such a bad start.

He swallowed and looked over at her while he tried to hold it all together. "He sounds like a good brother."

"He *was*." She looked up and right into David's eyes. "He was army—in Afghanistan. He died over there last year."

"I'm sorry." David stood there, wanting to comfort her, understanding her brother's need to take care of her. She was strong and tough, but David saw that essence of vulnerability in her pretty eyes and let go of his courage yet again. "We lost a lot of good soldiers. I'm sorry I couldn't save all of them."

I'm sorry I couldn't save your brother.

Compassion filled her eyes. "I'm sure you tried. You're one of the heroes, David. But you're home now, so take care of yourself."

David decided he had to tell her the truth soon. She'd be angry at him all over again, but he thought she was the kind of woman who'd respect the truth.

He took a deep breath. "Hey, listen, I—"

Whitney gave him a distracted, impatient stare. Then she blinked and stared at the clock on the console. "I'm sorry, but it's late and I've gotta go."

David shut the door and watched as she sped off along Desert Valley Drive. She couldn't get away from him fast enough. Or maybe she couldn't get away from the emotions he evoked in her. Too many bad memories. That was what he carried around, too.

How would she react when she found out he'd promised her brother he'd come here to see her? How could he keep her safe when she was so bent on taking care of herself?

It had to be done. He needed to let Whitney know that he'd tried to save Lucas. And that he'd promised Lucas he'd do this. Tomorrow, once he was settled and acclimated to his surroundings, he'd find her and talk to her.

He wasn't going anywhere for a few weeks at least. She'd get used to having him around. And he'd find a way to tell her exactly why he was here.

FOUR

David went inside the quaint inn, the chill of the dusk chasing him and the memory of Whitney cornered with a dangerous criminal still front and center in his mind.

"Well, you look plumb whipped," the petite gray-haired woman behind the counter said with a smile, her plump hands splayed across the old wood. "I'm Rosa. How can I help you?"

David explained that he needed a room for an indefinite time. "And where can I rent a car?"

The woman laughed at that, her pink bifocals slipping down on her nose. "Not around here, dear. But…I have a loaner you can use. All I ask is that you gas her up and keep her running smoothly."

David couldn't argue with that. "Deal."

Whitney pulled up to the small stucco house she rented from the Carters next door. When she'd first signed up for training last year, she'd stayed in the dorm-like condos next to the K9 Training Center. She'd met Shelby's father there, Brian Miller. Whitney had been a rookie in every way, naive and eager to fit in. When the handsome, charming fellow rookie had started flirting with her in spite of the no-fraternizing policy, she'd fallen hard.

Brian hadn't lived in the dorms, but he'd hung out there a lot. He'd had his own house between Desert Valley and another small town, about ten miles from the training center. He'd told her he preferred to live in his own place since he had a part-time job as a night watchman at a strip mall.

But she understood now, Brian had a house because he liked to take women there, where it was private and secluded. And apparently, he'd taken a lot of women there.

Brian had lied to her and cheated on her, even on the night before the police dance when she'd planned to tell him she was carrying his child. But then Brian had never made it to the dance. He'd died in a fire at his house about an hour before the dance started. Then, about two weeks later, her brother, Lucas, had been killed in Afghanistan.

Now Shelby would never know her daddy or her uncle. Whitney often wondered if Brian would have been happy to hear about the baby. Or would he have turned away from her?

She had no doubt Lucas would have loved Shelby, but he also would have made it his mission to come home and help Whitney out. She'd withheld telling him, and she'd paid dearly for that, too.

What did it matter now? Brian and her brother had both died too young. She knew how her brother had died. But she still didn't understand why or how Brian had died. Until lately, no one in the department had wanted to listen to the one theory that she couldn't shake. Had Brian been murdered?

Whitney glanced around, blinking. Night had settled in and with it, a desert chill. Every time she remembered Brian, the tug of a bittersweet struggle warred inside her soul. She'd loved him immediately. And he'd taken advantage of her completely. Now she had a beautiful baby girl and…because of Shelby, Whitney had turned her life around. She wanted to be worthy in her daughter's eyes, so she'd dedicated her life to Christ and made a pledge to be very careful regarding men. But even after all the pain of Brian's betrayal, Whitney still had concerns about how Brian had died.

In a house fire, supposedly from a burning candle.

His entire family had died in a horrible fire caused by a lit candle when he was a teenager.

He'd been the only survivor. So Brian never lit candles in his house. Ever.

It didn't make sense. But whenever she tried to explain that to people, they'd pat her on the hand and tell her the fire had been ruled as an accident. Whitney hoped to prove one day that the fire that had killed Brian had not been an accident. And since another rookie had died from a mysterious fall down the stairs of his home almost two years to the day before Brian died, she couldn't help but notice certain similarities. Couple that with Veronica Earnshaw's murder and the horrible murder of a police officer's wife five years ago and…things were being to look eerily similar.

But she couldn't think about that tonight. She needed to go next door and pick up Shelby. Marilyn Carter had four kids of her own, but she'd insisted on babysitting Shelby.

What's one more, honey? She'll fit right in and she'll learn a lot faster, watching my rug rats running around.

Whitney loved the Carters, and so did Shelby. She paid Marilyn what she could and thanked God each day for the family who had helped her change her life for the better.

She might be starting out with the department, but she loved her job, and she hoped like most of the rookies to move on to a big-city department one day. She wanted Shelby to have what she'd never had—stability.

"C'mon, Hunter," she said. "Here. Let's go find Shelby."

Whitney leashed the big dog and started toward her neighbors' rambling ranch house. But Hunter held back.

"What's wrong?" Whitney had never seen Hunter refusing to go next door. He loved the hustle and bustle of the crazy household full of children. He looked forward to seeing Shelby every day, too. "What's up, Hunter?"

He bristled and started growling low, a sure sign that something wasn't right. Whitney drew her weapon and ordered, "Go ahead."

Hunter tugged her toward the gate to her backyard, his growls now turning into aggressive barking. When Whitney rounded the corner, her heart picked up its tempo. The gate stood open, a broken latch dangling against it, the sound of the metal hitting wood grating on her nerves as a reminder that she'd messed with some dangerous people today.

Someone had broken into her backyard.

Releasing Hunter, Whitney ordered the K9 to search. Hunter took off, growling and barking. Whitney followed, thankful for the security light shining a sickly yellow glow over most of the small backyard. When Hunter alerted near the fence running along the back of the property, Whitney noticed some broken branches on a spindly pine sapling and some splintered areas on the weathered wood. Sneakers? Someone had hopped this fence. Ordering Hunter ahead of her, she quickly checked the house. The back door was locked, but she could tell from the scratches etched near the wood on the old lock that someone had been here and had tried to get into her house. She and Hunter had scared them away.

By the time she'd gathered herself enough to go next door to pick up Shelby, she saw Jack Carter standing out on the porch, squinting into the darkness.

"What's going on?" he asked, glancing at her house, his deep voice full of concern.

"A prowler, from what I could tell," she said, knowing the big, burly mechanic would watch the neighborhood if he thought someone was messing with them. But Whitney wanted to reassure her neighbor. She wouldn't put Jack and the family she trusted with her baby in danger. "Hunter will alert if they come back."

"It's getting as bad here as in the big towns," Jack said. "Want me to take a look?"

"No. I checked everything. The house is still locked tight. We arrived in time to keep them from getting inside."

"What do you think they wanted?" Jack asked, his hands on his hips.

She couldn't tell him her suspicions since she wasn't supposed to talk about an active case. It could get out around the neighborhood that drug dealers might be lurking in the area, and people might panic or, worse, take the law into their own hands. This could have been a coincidence, kids out for kicks. She hoped.

"I don't know," she said. "I don't have anything much of value in there." She glanced back at her tiny little rental home. The home she'd decorated with secondhand items. The home she loved even if it was a temporary place until she got her first assignment. It might be a rental, but it meant the world to her while she was still here in Desert Valley. "But would you tell Marilyn to give me a few more minutes? I want to check inside just in case."

"Sure," Jack said. "Shelby is on her play quilt giggling at the boys. She's fine."

Whitney nodded. She wanted to keep it that way, too. But as she made her way along with Hunter to the front door of the house, David Evans's words came back to her with full clarity, making Whitney wonder about those two men who'd gotten away earlier.

What if they come after you?

* * *

"I don't care what you think I should have done," Dr. William Pennington shouted to the scurrying nurse. "Get the gauze and let's get this man's finger sutured so I can get out of here on time for a change."

"I'll take care of Mr. Ramsey's cut," David told the teary-eyed nurse when she headed toward the supply room. The poor woman had been on her feet for over eight hours now. He'd arrived in town yesterday, and this was the first afternoon he'd volunteered here, but he hadn't seen any of the three nurses on staff take a real lunch break.

David enjoyed the work and being able to get to know some of the locals, but Whitney had been right. He couldn't see how anyone on earth would actually *want* to work for this tyrant of a physician. The man obviously thought he was above managing a run-down clinic in a small town. But he sure didn't make it easy to work for him, let alone volunteer.

Wondering if Whitney would make good on calling him in to look at mug shots, David hoped she'd been able to ID the two men without his help. He wanted to have another opportunity to talk to her, but not in a busy police station. He'd have to find a way to see her again and tell her that he'd known her brother, Lucas.

"Go ahead. Be my guest," the nurse whispered as she shoved the supplies into David's hands. David returned to the present, but the nurse was already leaving. "I'm outta here."

David watched her grab her purse and head for the back door, thinking his first day here had turned out to be exhausting. The doctor he'd talked to on the phone had seemed wary about someone offering to volunteer in the first place, but he'd also told David he could use the help. But in person, Dr. William Pennington was a harsh leader who barked orders and scared both nurses and patients. He'd guided David through the proper papers to allow him to practice medicine on a temporary volunteer basis, but he sure didn't seem appreciative of having an experienced volunteer on hand. Maybe he didn't want the staff to outshine him?

David had caught Dr. Pennington staring at him at odd moments. Maybe the man was territorial. His ego was as big as the whole state of Arizona. He stayed locked in his office between patients and talked in low growls on his cell when he paced up and down the hallway.

David intended to show the good doctor that he didn't scare that easily. He needed this work to keep him centered. He had a compulsion to help hurting people, a need that obviously stemmed from seeing too much death and destruction.

Or maybe from being the only son of a now deceased highly successful doctor who had been considered a pillar of the community back in East Texas. Could he ever live up to what his father had expected?

He returned to the exam room, where the doctor was fussing at the frazzled man who'd come in with a work-related injury. "You need to be more careful in that garage, Mr. Ramsey. This is the third work-related accident you've had in the past year."

"Couldn't be helped," the man said. "Wrench slipped. We're always backed up and behind. I got in a rush."

The condescending doctor with the gray-streaked dark hair stared down the grimy mechanic, his rimless glasses giving a clear view of his disapproval. "That doesn't mean you should get careless. I have my car serviced at Carter's Garage, you know. I'd hate to file a complaint with your boss because you failed to do your job correctly by being careless."

"Need some help?" David offered, smiling at the man who sat with a worried frown wrinkling his forehead.

"Where's Phyllis?" Dr. Pennington asked in a curt, angry tone, his scowl meant for David.

"I told her I'd help you out," David replied,

daring the doctor to say anything. "She never got her lunch break."

"All of my nurses know to take breaks," the doctor spouted. "Wait till I see her tomorrow. She also knows not to leave when we still have a patient. And you shouldn't be giving orders around here."

"I wasn't giving orders. I told her I'd help you," David repeated. "I'm here and I know what to do."

"Go home, Evans," the older doctor said, shaking his head as he glanced at David. "I still don't get why you're here in the first place." Grunting, he added, "I have my eye on you."

"I told you when I called," David said, preparing a care kit for Mr. Ramsey to take home with him. "I need something to do while I'm visiting, and since this is what I did as a medic, here I am." He eyed his surroundings, taking in the dents in the walls, the worn linoleum floors and the lack of needed supplies. "And it looks like you can use the help."

"Never enough time or help around here," Pennington retorted on a snarl. "And I sure can't pay you, so I hope you don't think your time here will count toward a permanent work situation."

"I'm volunteering," David reminded him,

anger simmering behind his politeness. "I don't expect pay."

But he did expect this man and the entire staff to show some respect to the patients. For the most part, the nurses were kind to anyone who came in. But they were so afraid of the doctor who ordered them around with angry comments and nasty expletives that they all had a serious morale problem.

"You must have some sort of motive, or a death wish," the doctor said to David. He stitched Mr. Ramsey's numbed finger without regard for the man's fearful expression. "Who'd purposely come here? Especially after serving for almost a year in Afghanistan."

David wondered about the doctor's question later when he was about to lock up the clinic for the day. But before he could bolt the front door of the old ranch-style building that must have once been a family home, the door burst open, and he stood face-to-face with Whitney Godwin. And she was carrying a crying baby girl.

FIVE

"David?"

She'd forgotten he'd offered to volunteer here. But it was too late to turn around and leave. Besides, she needed help, and in spite of not knowing David well, she did trust him for some strange reason.

"What's wrong?" he asked, his gaze moving over Shelby.

Getting over her shock, Whitney explained why *she* was here. She had nothing to hide after all. "My baby has a fever. It started last night. I think she's coming down with something, and I don't know what to do."

David replaced the look of complete surprise on his face with one of professional concern. "Okay, okay. Calm down. Let's get her into an exam room."

He guided Whitney down a short hallway and took her and Shelby into an empty, cold room. After he checked the examining table to make sure it had been cleared and cleaned, he turned back to Whitney. "Let's see if we can get her to lie still while I check her vitals."

She cooed at Shelby and tried to lay her on the table, but her daughter started sobbing all over again.

Whitney took a deep breath. She wouldn't fall apart in front of David Evans. If her day had gone according to plan, she would have called him to come back to the station for one more round of looking at mug shots. She was already in hot water with the chief for not calling for backup with the whole train fiasco, but he'd forgiven her when she'd produced the suspect's weapon and that shred of clothing. She'd barely had a chance to look at the mug books herself.

She'd gone back to work today, but the chief had put her on light duty since her ankle was still tender, a fact she tried to hide from everyone. But Carrie Dunleavy, the department secretary, had noticed her limping.

"I made cinnamon rolls," Carrie had said. "Thought everyone could use something sweet with all of this going on. Go sit in the break room and put your foot up. I'll bring you one with some coffee."

Whitney had accepted the delicious roll, but she'd stayed at her desk to make calls to sort real tips from false ones. They needed witnesses to help piece together the lead K9 trainer's murder and to find Marco, the missing German shepherd puppy that had disappeared from the training yard the night of her death.

Whitney might be sore and bruised, but she wasn't one to give up.

Today, she'd been teamed again with officer Eddie Harmon to run down some leads, most of which were either crazy people wanting attention or curious people hoping to make the news, since a reporter from the *Canyon County Gazette* had been snooping around. Tracking those two low-level criminals from the train had taken a backseat.

But Whitney sure would have liked to collar them and find another shipment of heroin to prove her case. If what David Evans had seen was correct, that much heroin would be worth a lot of money on the street. As in thousands of dollars.

When Shelby started crying again, she forgot about her workload and returned her attention to David. "She woke up around three this morning, fussy and crying. I gave her some drops for the fever and rocked her back to sleep. She seemed better this morning when I left her with the babysitter."

David nodded and spoke softly to Shelby. He

managed to check her ears while Whitney held her, but Shelby wasn't happy with that, either.

"Is she okay?" she asked, praying Shelby just had a bit of a cold. Was she old enough to be teething? Whitney wished she'd reread all the help books well-meaning people had given her.

"I think she'll be fine," David said. "Let me check a few other things." He gave Whitney a reassuring smile. Then he started with the standard questions. "How old is she?"

"Five months. Closer to six, really."

"Is she eating properly?"

"Yes. Formula and some baby food."

"Any other illnesses or problems recently?"

"No. Nothing." Whitney patted Shelby's little back. "She's usually a happy, healthy baby."

She wanted him to understand, so Whitney started with nervous chatter, trying to explain, trying to show that she was a good mother. "I work such crazy hours, but I have a great babysitter right next door. Marilyn. She has four boys. She thinks it might be an ear infection."

"She might be right," David said, his tone professional and sure. "An experienced mother usually knows her stuff."

And she wasn't that experienced, Whitney thought. She should have stayed at home today. How could she leave her sick child with someone else? How could she do this? Love someone so much it hurt to breathe whenever her baby was hurting?

How could she take care of Shelby and do the kind of work her job demanded?

Tired and bleary-eyed, Whitney had gone on to work after Marilyn had promised she'd call if Shelby got cranky again. When Marilyn called later in the day and told her Shelby had a fever and it was climbing, Whitney had rushed home in time to get Shelby to the clinic.

"She'd never been this sick before," she said, trying to hold tight to her emotions. "Marilyn suggested I bring her here since I'd never make it to the pediatrician's office before it closes. It's about twenty miles west of here in the Canyon County Medical Center."

"You did the right thing," David said, his voice soothing, his eyes on Shelby. He placed a thermometer inside Shelby's little ear. Which the baby didn't like at all.

"She has a high fever," he said after reading the thermometer. "One-oh-three."

Whitney inhaled and wished she could be a better mother. "It was close to a hundred and two the last time Marilyn checked. She didn't want to give her any more medicine until I got home."

"We'll give her something to bring it down," David said. "What's her name?"

"Shelby," Whitney said, her heart breaking with each little whimper.

David took over, checking Shelby and cooing to her in a way that helped Whitney relax. Shelby actually started smiling at his antics. Whitney smiled, too, but it didn't relieve her apprehension.

She felt guilty for spending the day checking leads and trying to figure out angles on Veronica Earnshaw's murder at the K9 Training Center. Whitney wished she could get the case out of her mind. But they all wondered why one of the puppies Veronica had been working with when she'd been killed had gone missing. Chief Jones wanted this case solved. And so did a lot of prominent people who'd helped sponsor the whole puppy program. Today they'd at least tracked down leads on witnesses who'd said they'd seen a puppy running along Desert Valley Road the night Veronica had been murdered. Whitney had reported her prowler to the chief, too. She didn't need a drug lord gunning for her. She had to protect Shelby, no matter what.

Torn between doing her job and taking care of her baby, Whitney tried to focus on the here and now.

"Okay, Shelby," David said, his expression hard to read. "We're going to make you feel better."

Shelby laughed and then reached up for her mother. After Whitney took her, she buried her little head against Whitney's blue uniform collar and started bawling all over again.

Whitney heard footsteps stalking up the hallway. Dr. Pennington charged into the room, his face red with rage. "What's going on here? I was on my way out the door."

When he saw Whitney standing there, he looked shocked, but a cautious blankness wiped his surprise away. "Oh, Officer Godwin. What are you doing here?"

Whitney wanted to drop through the floor. She'd never cared for Dr. Pennington, but she tried to tolerate him since he'd once been married to Veronica Earnshaw. But she refused to succumb to the shame she'd felt after he'd insulted her when she'd become pregnant and had remained husbandless. At least he hadn't spread the word when she'd come to him as a patient last year, since he couldn't break confidentiality.

Straightening her spine, she held Shelby tight. "We're almost done."

"Her little girl is sick," David said on a sharp note before Whitney could say more. "You can leave, Doc. I've got it."

The cantankerous doctor glanced from David back to Whitney. "Stop ordering me around, Evans. You've only been here one day, and this is still my clinic." He tried to take Shelby, but the baby started crying again. "What seems to be the problem?"

"A high fever," David said. "I've checked her ears. She has some congestion in her chest, too."

"She's been cranky," Whitney said, gently holding Shelby still while David listened to Shelby's heart. "She was congested last night."

The doctor scrubbed a hand down his face. "Could be allergies or she might be teething."

Whitney watched in amazement as David ignored the doctor and went about examining Shelby. Most people cowered when Dr. Pennington entered a room. He was a known bully around here. She'd brought Shelby here only because she was so worried. She'd take Shelby to her regular doctor for a second opinion, just to be sure. Right now, she had to trust David and Dr. Pennington.

Together, they checked Shelby over, both silent and seeming determined to make the proper diagnosis. Whitney even sensed a begrudging respect for David in Dr. Pennington's silvery eyes.

"She has an ear infection," David finally announced.

"And she's teething," the doctor said, his tone grumpy but low-key. "We'll prescribe antibiotics and something for the fever."

"Will she be all right?" Whitney asked, more frightened of something happening to Shelby than she'd ever been of dealing with dangerous criminals.

David gave her an encouraging glance. "She'll be better soon. This is normal at five months." His expression changed to something she couldn't quite figure out. He was probably wondering if she had a husband. Whitney hoped he wouldn't ask.

After locking up, David walked Whitney to her police vehicle. While she put a drowsy little Shelby in the baby seat, he glanced in the back. "Where's Hunter?"

Whitney hurried to find her keys. "I left him at my house, and I need to get back." She couldn't thank David enough, but she turned to tell him once again.

He spoke before she could show him her gratitude. "I'll follow you home and make sure Shelby is okay. I mean, until your husband gets home. Or is he already there?"

"You don't have to do that." Whitney's surprise turned to anger. "And I don't have a husband. It's just Shelby and me."

Maybe she shouldn't have told him that. She didn't know him and his reasons for being here were a bit sketchy. He could be the one who'd tried to break into her house. Besides, he probably didn't even have a car.

"I wasn't trying to be nosy," David said. "I wanted to check up on you today, but I got busy here. Any word on those two goons?"

"No, and I can't discuss that with you right now. Sorry I didn't call you with an update."

She whirled and opened the driver's-side door. "As for me, I told you, I can take care of myself. Thank you for checking over my baby, but I have to get her home."

David didn't make a move to let her leave. "Look, I need to talk to you about something important."

Whitney's instincts kicked in, making her wonder what this man was doing in Desert Valley and why he'd volunteered to work at the clinic. But in spite of her doubts, she believed David Evans was a good man. He had come to her rescue yesterday, and she appreciated that. She couldn't be careless like that again. She had to think of Shelby.

"What is it?" she asked David, hoping she wouldn't regret trusting this man. In spite of that fragile trust, she had to be firm with him. "I told you, I'm okay. I've been on my own for a long time. So you don't need to—"

He put a hand on the open door of her car, his brown eyes reminding her of the desert at dusk. "You're right. You don't know me, Whitney. But...I knew your brother. I knew Lucas. And that's why I'm here."

SIX

Whitney dropped her car keys onto the seat. "What did you say?"

David held the door, his expression full of sympathy and regret. "I served with Lucas. I was assigned to his unit."

Whitney swayed on her feet. Putting a hand to her temple, she said, "No. That can't be possible. He never mentioned you."

David held her, his hand on her arm. "It's true. I wanted to tell you right away, but everything got so crazy."

Now she was mad. Pushing him away, she glanced back at Shelby and then whirled, still trying to absorb what he'd just admitted. "So when were you going to tell me, David? You've been here a couple of days now."

He nodded. "Yes…and I've been threatened, held at gunpoint and interrogated at the police station. Not a good time to blurt out something like that. Then today I headed to the clinic to get a tour, but I got busy helping the crowd in the waiting room. I planned on calling you tonight."

"After you *volunteered* in this clinic today," she pointed out. "If I hadn't run into you here, I don't think you would have told me at all."

"I planned on telling you tonight," he repeated. "Look, it's been kind of wild since I got here. I had to get settled and I had to get things straight in my head. This wasn't easy, coming here right after I got back stateside. But I'm here, and I'm willing to explain."

"Yeah, well, you do have a lot to explain."

She'd had more than enough of dishonest men in her life, but she also yearned for any information regarding her brother. Her anger misted into an intense pain that she didn't want David to see. Turning to grab her keys, she said, "I need to get Shelby home and into bed."

"Wait." David held the door again. "Lucas made me promise, Whitney. His last words were about you."

Whitney's anger and despair dispersed like a mirage floating out over the horizon. Tears pricked at her eyes. "What…what did he say?"

David touched her arm again, this time to comfort her. "He said a lot of things, but mostly that you were strong and tough, but he'd feel better knowing someone was looking out for you."

She blinked and took in a breath. "And he picked you for that task?"

David's smile was soft and bittersweet. "Yeah, for some reason he believed in me."

Shelby whimpered and held out her arms. Whitney wiped at the tears in her eyes, but she wouldn't fall apart in front of her baby. "Why don't you follow me home so we can talk, okay?"

David let out a breath. "Good idea. I'll be right behind you."

She nodded, and wondered if that statement meant for longer than tonight. "Lucas," she whispered as she slowly drove home, her heart breaking. "What have you done?"

Thankful that the rusty yellow vintage Chevy truck Miss Rosa loaned him had made it across town, David stood in front of the tiny fireplace, staring at the unburned logs Whitney had placed there, while Hunter lay by the table, staring at David. The stucco house was tiny and neat with a minimalist decor that spoke of Whitney's efficiency. A floral couch with deep cushions and one lone blue chair by the hearth. A small round coffee table holding magazines and a green plant centered in front of the couch. A few pretty pictures and decorative mirrors scattered on the cream-colored walls.

On a side table, he spotted a picture of Shelby as a newborn. Then he noticed some sort of colorful contraption in the corner that had all kinds of fun toy attachments to entice a baby.

Hunter had his own bed, too, near the fireplace.

The sleek dog stared up at David with eyes that wanted to like him, but David was pretty sure Hunter was waiting for the next command. Or maybe his next meal. David hoped it would be dog food and not his arm or leg.

"We'll get to know each other more," David told Hunter. "Just you wait. We'll be best friends soon."

Hunter didn't move, but his ears perked up.

David took another glance at the baby picture. A little girl dressed in white and pink. Tiny. So tiny.

Whitney had a five-month-old baby. Born in November of last year, if David's calculations were correct. If Lucas had known before he died, he'd never mentioned it. Had he withheld that particular bit of information for a reason?

David couldn't judge Whitney, but he sure was curious. To hide that curiosity, he studied the rest of the house and hoped he'd find some clues. Hunter's gaze followed him as he strolled around the long rectangular room.

Across from the fireplace wall, a small kitchen

island with two tall stools opened to the white-and-blue kitchen and a side door to the carport.

Down the short hallway where she'd taken Shelby, he'd noticed what had to be two bedrooms with a bath centered between them. Simple and clean.

He figured Whitney was a bit more complex and intriguing than anyone knew, and he had a feeling he'd see a different side of her once she got Shelby all tucked in.

When he heard her coming back up the hallway, he noticed her faded jeans and white T-shirt. Her personal dress code must be efficient, too. But that long, shiny blond hair made her all woman. She probably had no idea that the casual outfit and loose mane of hair made her look attractive. Way too attractive.

She gave him a wary glance as she headed barefoot to the kitchen. Then she called to Hunter. The dog came trotting, his brown eyes giving Whitney an adoring stare. He was an impressive animal with a pretty white coat spotted with tan.

After feeding Hunter and giving him clean water, she turned to David. "I have water, soda and coffee."

"Coffee," he said. It had been a long day.

She reached for the coffeemaker, and he

walked over to a bar stool and sat down. "So...
you trained here and now you live here?"

She didn't look ready to divulge anything, but
she finally said, "Yes. I lived in the dorms—a
big condo located near the training center—last
year when I first came here to train. But I had
to drop out when I got pregnant."

"Did Lucas know?"

Her expression turned somber. "He died before I could tell him. I was in my first trimes-
ter."

"Okay, that explains that."

"It was hard, burying my brother when I had
a new life inside me." She shook her hair off her
face as if to shake away the grief. "But I managed to keep going. I had to, for Shelby's sake."

And she was doing that now, he thought.

"I've waffled between regret for not letting
him know sooner and relief that he never knew.
Lucas would have moved heaven and earth to
come home, and I didn't want him to jeopardize
his military career on my account." She stared
down at the counter. "But he might be alive
today if I'd told him about the baby. He would
have found a way to come home."

The torment in her eyes ripped through David's heart. He knew all about that kind of guilt
and regret. "You couldn't have predicted this,
Whitney. I know it sounds pat, but he was doing

what he loved, and he was good at it. He wanted you to feel the same about becoming a police officer."

"I do," she said. "So much so that I came back to try again, and now I'm renting this house from the people next door. The Carters. Marilyn is my babysitter, and her husband's a mechanic. He owns a garage here in town. I owe them a lot. They encouraged me to go to church with them, and I'm glad I did."

"That's good," David said, relieved that she had decent people in her life to help her out. "So you came back to start over, but you couldn't live in the dorms with a baby."

"Right. I'm only here temporarily. We all got involved in a big murder case right after we graduated, so our assignments to police stations across the state have been put on hold. One of our own was killed. Our master dog trainer, Veronica Earnshaw, was found dead near a gate to the puppy yard. Someone shot her. We were all in shock, and then the chief explained we'd been put on retainer by one of our wealthy donors, Marian Foxcroft. You met her daughter, Ellen, yesterday. We were all ordered to stay here and help solve not only Veronica's murder but also the suspicious deaths of two rookies and the murder of an officer's wife five years ago. That officer had been a rookie at the time."

"Wow." David could see the stress and strain in her eyes, but he was glad she'd be hanging around for a while. And he sure wasn't leaving now, either. "How long are you staying?"

"Indefinitely," she said. "I've extended my lease here for another month."

One month. He would probably be gone after that anyway.

"Where do you want to go once this is over?"

She busied herself with measuring coffee into the filter cup. "I'm from Tucson, so I'd like to go back there. But you probably already know about Tucson. My mother and Lucas are both buried there."

He listened, treading carefully. Did those two men from yesterday have anything to do with the murder case? He knew she couldn't reveal details to a civilian, but he wondered if she was in danger from more than one source.

He'd talk about her brother for now since that was why she'd let him follow her home. "Lucas told me he was from Arizona, but he never mentioned Tucson. He said his family moved around a lot."

David had confided in Lucas about his own deceased parents, too. They'd had that in common. But now wasn't the time to mention that to Whitney.

She hit the brew button on the tiny coffeepot and then started putting away clean dishes from the drainer sitting by the sink. "Yes, we went from base to base, but we finally settled in Tucson. Our dad was military, too. He was wounded in Desert Storm not long after I was born and came home and later died of heart disease. He and our mother divorced when I was around ten, and she never remarried. She died of breast cancer about five years ago."

David didn't know what to say. "Lucas didn't talk much about that, but I knew your parents were both dead. He said you were his only close relative."

She took two bright red coffee cups out of a cabinet. "He had a hard time with it since he was the eldest. He was twenty and I was only fifteen when Dad had a massive heart attack." She brought the coffee over, pulled out what looked like homemade muffins and handed him one. Blueberry. "After Mom died, Lucas became the typical protective brother."

David smiled. "You mean overbearing and always bossy but also loyal and fearless?"

She nodded and nibbled on her muffin, then turned to pull some leftover cold chicken out of the fridge. "Yes, you do know my brother. He vetted all of my boyfriends. It got worse when he joined up. I was out on my own by then… but he always worried about me."

"He was proud of you," David said. "He worried about your choice of professions, but he loved you. And he came around on the whole K9 officer thing in the end."

"He told you about that?"

David saw the rush of embarrassment in her eyes. She seemed to value her privacy. "He needed to vent a little. Lucas was like that. He had to figure out things on his own terms."

"Yes, we're alike in that respect," she said with a wry smile.

"I'm gathering that."

"I guess this is kind of weird for you." She stared across at him. "I can't believe he made you promise to come here. And frankly, I can't understand why you *are* here."

"Isn't that obvious?" David asked, the baked chicken reminding him that he was starving. He had to smile at Hunter. The dog lifted his nose in the air. Maybe he liked chicken, too.

"Nothing about this is obvious," she retorted as she shredded the meat and handed him a plate. "Why are you here?"

She had the direct-questioning thing down. He pitied anyone who had the misfortune of being interrogated by her. She stared at him with a blue-eyed vengeance.

David didn't know how to explain. "I made

a promise to a dying soldier," he said. "But... Lucas was also my friend."

Her eyes looked like a cloudy sky. "So you always keep your promises?"

David realized one thing, sitting there with her. Lucas might have sent him here, but Whitney would be the reason he'd stay. "I try," he said. Then he bit into the tender chicken.

"Finish eating," she told him. "And then you and I are going to have a serious discussion."

Whitney stared at her reflection in the bathroom mirror. She wouldn't give in to the tears or the regrets or the frustration. Nothing could bring back all the people she'd lost. Her parents, her brother, the father of her child.

And now she had to deal with a man who'd traveled around the world to find her.

Unbelievable. The odds of that same man being all tangled up as a witness to a possible drug smuggling ring were hard to imagine. It only forced them together—for now.

Of all the trains in all the towns...

He had to be on that particular one.

He could have been killed, and then she would never have known about her brother's last hours.

So she looked at herself in the mirror and decided to get over being angry at David. She should be thankful that he'd been so determined to find her. And that, like her brother, he was a true gentleman and a protector.

He's a good man. A kind, caring man who helped save a lot of lives during the worst of circumstances. He tried to save my brother. He tried to help me.

And David was probably feeling a lot of guilt pangs, too.

She could do this. She could go back out there and let him talk, just talk. And maybe she'd finally be able to talk about her life, too. It would be nice to share things with someone who would be out of her life soon anyway. No repercussions. No drama. If she didn't count the facts that he'd known Lucas and that he'd come a long way to honor her brother's wishes.

Time to find out a little bit more about her new protector.

But when she opened the bathroom door, she heard Hunter emitting a low, dangerous growl. Thinking he might have David pinned against a wall, she rounded the corner. "Hey—"

David wasn't anywhere in the living room or kitchen. And the door to the carport was standing open.

Hunter gave her a let's-roll glance and alerted. Something was definitely going on out there.

Going to the hall closet, Whitney unlocked

her gun box and hurried to the open door. "David?" she called in a low whisper. "David, are you out there?"

SEVEN

David knew he wasn't imagining things.

When he'd glanced out the back window, he'd seen a shadow in the backyard. A movement there in the moonlight. Maybe a tree? But then he'd heard a commotion, too. Without thinking, he'd opened the carport door and hurried around the corner of the house.

Now he could hear Hunter's growls. Whitney would wonder what had happened. When he heard footsteps, he stopped behind a tree. Then a light switched on, and he heard Whitney commanding Hunter.

"Go. Find."

The dog leaped into the air, barking and snarling as he took off toward the back fence. David saw a dark figure running out from behind a cluster of bushes, and then he heard the old fence creaking and groaning. Hurrying to where Hunter stood barking, David saw a sneakered foot making it over the shoulder-high enclosure.

"Stop," Whitney called as she came running.

David figured she had her gun on *him*. He turned. "It's me."

"I know it's you. And I know you well enough now to think you might sail over that fence right after whoever that was in my yard."

She had him there. "Yep. Hunter saw him, too."

Whitney slowly made her way toward him, her gun held down at her side. "Probably the same person who broke the lock on my gate when I got home last night."

"What?" David whirled to stare at her. "Someone was here? Was it the drug smugglers?"

She let out a sigh. "I don't know. Hunter alerted when we got home. But I checked and didn't find anyone."

"Did you tell your chief or anyone else about this?"

"Yes," she said in a defensive tone. "I thought it might be kids. We have a lot of teens always wandering around here."

"And you had a run-in with drug smugglers that same day," he reminded her. "It could have been one of them."

She stalked around the small yard. "I know."

"We both saw them up close. They might want to wipe that little scene *and* us out of their minds."

"I have Hunter, and I'd never put Shelby in danger but I do have to be alert until we find them." Then she let out a breath. "Shelby. I have to get back inside."

David watched as she took off, Hunter behind her.

He checked the fence, touching it and pushing on it. It was wobbly and old, and that was probably what he'd heard earlier when someone tried to climb over. He could fix that. Her landlord next door needed to do something about this, but David could take care of it and solve the problem for all of them.

After making sure no one else was around, he started toward the house. When he heard a car cranking up down the street, he had a feeling that the intruder was once again getting away.

When he came inside, Whitney was sitting on the couch, her gun lying on the table beside her.

Glancing around, he asked, "Is Shelby okay?"

"She's asleep. Her room is safe."

"Did you report this?"

"I'm the police, remember?"

"Yeah. I can see that. But…you're not safe."

"I have my weapon and a trained partner."

Hunter sat at her feet as if to prove that point.

David wanted to prove *his* point. "Yeah, well, now you have me, too."

Whitney held up one hand. "Oh, no. No, I

don't. You've done what you came here to do. You don't have to stick around on my account."

Because no one else had, apparently.

"I said, I'm not leaving."

"You mean, tonight? Or tomorrow? Or never?"

"That all depends. You've got a lot going on. A baby to take care of, drug smugglers hounding you and some big murder case you can't talk much about."

Her blue eyes shot fire. "That's right. That's my job."

"Well, whether you like it or not, you and I are involved in what happened yesterday. Together. We were there together."

"And whether you like it or not, I have to investigate, and I will find out what's going on. You only need to take care of yourself. Not me. I'm not holding you to that misguided promise my brother guilted you into."

David stood in front of the fireplace while she stayed on the couch. "Why are you so stubborn?"

"Why are you so determined to be my knight in shining armor?"

He wanted to tell her that he'd promised. But mainly, he wanted to assure her that he would stick around whether she liked it or not. He almost told her, because even though they'd had some odd, trying moments together so far, he liked her.

But she wasn't ready for a showdown right now. Or anything else.

"I don't want to be anybody's hero," he finally said. "I'm in this, Whitney. Whether you like it or not, I'm on those two criminals' list right along with you. Why don't we work together to bring them to justice?"

She gave him a stubborn pout and then tugged at her hair. "I want justice," she said. "For all of them."

"What do you mean, for all of them?"

She let out a sigh and stood up. "I don't know if the person who came into my backyard has to do with the alleged drug trafficking through this town or…if it has to do with several people I know possibly being murdered. But one way or another, I intend to find out."

A few minutes later, David gave up trying to figure out this case. But he didn't want to go back to the inn just yet. "I guess you want me to leave, right?"

Whitney didn't know what she wanted. Yesterday, David Evans had been an eyewitness to a strange drug-smuggling operation and a stabbing. Today, he had become so much more. The medic who'd tried to save her brother and helped her baby, and a man who'd traveled a long way to honor a promise.

Now she longed to know everything, including his history.

When she didn't respond, he added, "I know you can't talk about your work, so I won't ask you to explain that earlier comment about possible murders, but I'd like to know more about you."

"It is getting late, but…David…we've talked about me a lot. Let's get back to you."

"Are you asking as a police officer?" His brown eyes grew daring. "Or as a friend?"

Surprised, she let out a breath. "Are we friends?"

"I'd like to think so," he said. Settling into the old chair she'd found at a flea market and recovered in a denim blue, he scrubbed a hand down his five-o'clock shadow. "I mean, doesn't being attacked and almost shot make people BFFs?"

Whitney laughed at that. And realized it had been a while since she'd had a good laugh. "I would think so, yes. Best friends forever."

Then she looked up and into his eyes and really saw *him*.

As a man. A very attractive man, sitting here in her living room late at night. She remembered how a scene very much like this one had gotten her into a lot of hot water just over a year ago.

Trouble.

She didn't need any more trouble.

She loved Shelby and thanked God every day for her sweet little girl. But next time she wanted to fall in love by the book. Faith, hope and love. That was what she wanted next time.

And in that order.

"Hey, you don't have to be my best friend," he said, misunderstanding her sudden silence. "I'll settle for being new friends right now."

"I'm thinking," she admitted. "I'd like to get to know you a little better."

He smiled and tapped his fingers against the chair. "I lost both my parents, too," he said, his tone quiet.

"What?"

"They were killed in a car wreck two years ago. I was inside a triage tent at a field hospital, trying to convince a dying soldier that he would be okay. He had a hole in his gut that no amount of morphine or surgery would ever relieve."

Whitney gulped in air and then put her hand to her mouth. "David, I'm so sorry."

"My father suffered a massive heart attack while they were heading down a country road, admiring the wildflower trails in the Texas Hill Country. The car ran off the road and hit a tree. It's fitting that they died together. They loved each other so much. I was their only child. I became a medic because of my father. He was a surgeon."

Whitney sat there, thinking how blessed they'd both been in their lives—and yet they'd both suffered tragedies, too. "Did he…know what you'd done? Saving so many, trying to comfort those who wouldn't make it?"

"He knew. He was proud of me, but he kind of planned for me to follow in his footsteps. I wanted to open a family practice and he fussed at me, telling me I'd be overworked and underpaid. Then, when I joined the army, he…he changed. He was full of resolve and accepted my choices, but I think he was waiting for me to come home and settle down. He worried that something would happen to me. His legacy was the most important thing in the world to him, and I was supposed to be a big part of that."

"You felt guilty because you weren't there, right?"

She could see it in his eyes. Feel it whenever he heaved a shuddering breath. The same guilt she felt whenever she thought of Brian and her brother.

"Yes. I might have seen the signs, or I could have cautioned him to slow down and take it easy. He volunteered a lot—clinics and mission trips and homeless shelters. He had a true servant's heart."

Now she understood what made David Evans tick. Coming here to see her, immediately volunteering at the clinic that always needed extra hands, sitting with the injured train attendant and even staying with her at the train scene until he knew she was safe. David was trying to measure up to his father's expectations. But he also had a servant's heart. He cared about people, and he wasn't like that just to measure up to someone else's legacy. He's made his own legacy by being a good man.

"I think you might be that way, too," she said, seeing him in a whole new light. "And I think your father would be proud that the Evans legacy will live on…in you."

"I guess so." He smiled again. "Didn't mean to be a downer. I wanted you to know that I understand how you feel. It's tough, going it alone. But you and I… We're survivors."

"Yes." They could agree on that, at least.

"I should go," he said, getting up in a slow, lanky way that made her want him to stay a while longer. "But…are you sure you'll be okay?"

"I'm fine, David," she replied, appreciating him more now that they'd talked. "I have security lights, and I have Hunter to alert me. Shelby's window has a solid lock on it. The house is small and secure. And I have the Carters right next door."

"Plus, you are a highly trained police officer."

"Twice trained," she quipped, feeling good about him but a little anxious about whoever kept coming into her yard. But she wouldn't tell David that. He'd sleep on the couch if it meant fulfilling his duty.

He started toward the front door and then pivoted. "Hey, I can at least check on Shelby and see if her fever's broken."

"Good idea. You are highly trained, right?"

"Right." He grinned. "I've seen it all, too."

"Yes, and you'll see everything at the clinic. Be careful around Dr. Pennington. He was married to Veronica, just so you know. He's still bitter because she left him for another man. He hates it here and he'd like nothing more than to get hired on at some big city hospital. And… he's kind of territorial. I'm surprised he even accepted your offer to volunteer."

"I did notice he likes to call the shots, but when I walked in today, he didn't have time to argue with me. I think his entire staff would be glad if he'd find another position," David said. "But don't worry. I'll watch my back."

While he was watching her back, Whitney thought.

She guided him back to Shelby's nursery, which she'd decorated in soft pinks and bright greens. Her sweet baby was sleeping peacefully, her flowers-and-frogs mobile floating over the bed.

Whitney watched as David leaned over the white crib and touched a big, tanned hand to Shelby's brow. Seeing him there reminded her of how she'd often imagined Brian, Shelby's father, there. But David wasn't Brian, and nothing could change that.

David was different. Strong, noble, caring, willing to sacrifice for others. He touched Shelby in a way that showed he cared. This scene touched Whitney in places that had long gone dormant.

Whitney's brittle heart seemed to soften like a dry desert flower opening up to a soaking rain.

Faith, hope and love.

She wanted those things.

Now more than ever.

But first, she had to solve a murder. She needed to find out who killed Veronica and the others. Especially who killed Brian Miller. Maybe Marian Foxcroft was right to want these incidents declared accidents, but Whitney's gut told her differently. Maybe all of these murders were connected.

EIGHT

Two days later, Whitney was once again on the job and feeling better. Shelby had improved after a day at home, where Whitney made some cold calls regarding Veronica's murder, hoping to follow up on some tips that had come into the station. Marilyn had promised to call if Shelby had any problems. Whitney was still learning how to balance work with having a baby to care for, but knowing Marilyn would alert her if Shelby needed her helped a lot to ease her mind.

Now, after a day of chasing down more leads that hadn't panned out, Whitney was back with Eddie Harmon again. Chief Jones liked to pair the rookies with older, more experienced police officers, and that was all fine and good.

But Eddie wasn't the best mentor. He wasn't focused on the job anymore, and he didn't care that someone had shot Veronica. While she'd angered a lot of people and she'd been hard to deal with, Veronica didn't deserve to die the way she had. But Eddie didn't seem too concerned about finding her killer. He only wanted to work the beat and go home early. Still smarting from his wisecracks about her at the train scene the other day, Whitney planned to ignore Eddie and do what she had to do.

"I want you two to interview Veronica's ex-husband, Dr. Pennington, again," Chief Jones said, his towering height intimidating Whitney.

"I thought he'd already been interviewed," Eddie whined. "I can't deal with that sorry—"

"Careful," the chief cautioned. "Let me explain, Eddie." He turned to Whitney, silently assigning her as point person when he gave her a direct nod. "The doctor was interviewed a few weeks ago, but I need you to ask him one more time if he can think of anyone else who had it in for Veronica. I've heard that they argued about a lot of things, that maybe Veronica was making demands on the doctor's finances. We've asked questions, yes, but we need to narrow this down and see if he slips up on something. We keep asking until we hit on something. Or notice something that might be off a little bit."

"Half the town had it in for that woman," Eddie said, his massive hands on his hips.

"Then, you interview half the town," the chief

replied, his piercing eyes daring Eddie to say another word.

"We'll take care of it, sir," Whitney said. She turned and headed out, not waiting for Eddie to get in gear.

"Hey, Godwin!"

She turned back at the chief's call, almost running into the always-in-a-hurry department secretary, Carrie Dunleavy.

"Sorry," Carrie said, her brown eyes behind horn-rimmed glasses, a stack of files in her hands.

"That's okay," Whitney replied with a smile. Carrie took care of a lot of details around here. Scooting around Carrie, she said, "Yes, sir."

"What's the status on our eyewitness—David Evans?"

That she could answer. "His background check came back clean. He was deployed for nine months this past tour, and he's only been back stateside for a couple of months. No record, not even a traffic ticket. Grew up in Texas, played football and baseball in high school and was top of his class in college and med school. Made sure he had all the proper paperwork in check to volunteer at the clinic while he's here."

David was one of the good guys.

The chief nodded. "We haven't found any vehicles matching the partial plates Evans remembered, but Louise is still searching for the emblem you and your witness described. No word from the lab in Flagstaff regarding the fabric from the suspect's pants. Hope to hear on the weapon later today."

"Thanks, sir," Whitney replied. "We'll get on with these leads. Oh, and the railroad station manager said we could take a look at the video cameras at the station sometime this week."

"All right. Get out there and get at it," Chief Jones said, waving her away.

The department secretary, back at her desk, called out, "Hey, how's Shelby?"

"Much better, thankfully," Whitney replied.

"You work too hard," Carrie replied with an appreciative smile. "But you're good at it. Sooner or later, the person who did this will slip up. I hope you get a chance to be in on finding out the truth."

Whitney wanted that chance, too. "Thanks, Carrie."

Carrie smiled. "Hey, do you have a date for the dance next month?"

Whitney thought of David. "Nah, I'll probably go solo."

"Welcome to my world," Carrie said on a wistful note. "I'll probably be by myself again."

Hoping to encourage the shy woman, Whitney said, "Well, you never know. Someone might surprise you and ask to be your date."

"From your mouth to God's ear," Carrie said as she walked away.

Carrie was single like Whitney, so they often compared notes on everything from plants to fashion. Not that either of them looked like supermodels. But it was good to have someone to talk to now and then. Next time Whitney got the female rookies and trainers together for a girls' night out, she'd have to invite Carrie.

As she headed out the door, she refocused and wished Eddie would go ahead and retire, since he wanted to do that anyway. He made it known all the time that he was ready to spend more time with his family. Whitney didn't have that luxury, however. So she had to follow orders.

"Chief Jones is determined to find a killer," Eddie said once he was in the car. His aggravation showed as he yanked the seat belt on the passenger side of the patrol car and made sure it clicked.

"We all want to find Veronica's killer," Whitney countered. "Not to mention investigating Melanie's murder and the two other deaths."

"You mean Mike and Brian?" Eddie shook his head. "Both ruled accidents. Need to let that go, girl."

"I'm not letting anything go," Whitney said.

"It's all too coincidental, Eddie. Surely you have to agree with that."

"Yeah, I guess so." He gave her a sheepish glance. "Don't mind me. I should be more encouraging to a rookie. It's just that sometimes all the politics and red tape get to me. It's frustrating to see the truth right there and not find any evidence to substantiate it."

Hunter sat in the back, staring at Eddie as if he was trying to figure him out. But Whitney could understand Eddie's frustration. Police work was tedious at times.

"We have to do our jobs," Whitney reminded him, hoping to get him enthused and involved. "We don't have to like Veronica, but we do have an obligation to find out who killed her."

"Right." Eddie chuckled. "All you rookies, so eager to please. Does the chief throw you treats, too?" He grinned to soften that remark.

Whitney changed lanes and said, "Let's get this over with so I can make it home at a decent hour right along with you."

He chuckled again, but he did shut up. Eddie liked to get home as early as possible so he could watch sports and boss his overworked wife around. The poor woman had four kids of various ages to take care of. She carted them all over town for sports events and dance classes, and he wanted to be there for all of it. Admirable in a sweet kind of way. He did brag on his children, so Whitney knew he loved them.

Five minutes later, Whitney pulled the car into the big, rambling house that had been re-zoned commercial and now served as Desert Valley Clinic. Remembering that she might run into David there, she took a deep breath and made a solemn pledge to herself to concentrate on doing her job.

But when they entered the clinic, it was chaos, as usual. A lot of the people around there didn't have well-paying jobs, let alone insurance. This was the only place they could come. Several patients sat in the waiting room. They all looked up when they saw a K9 officer with a dog coming through the doors.

Hunter sniffed the air but didn't alert, thankfully. She never knew whom she'd find waiting in the overworked clinic. And since the train fiasco had been on the evening news, she was sure everyone around here was a little jittery.

"I hate this place," Eddie said in a loud whisper. "Hot and stinking."

Whitney wanted to tell him to get a better attitude since *his* deodorant had stopped working around noon, but she kept moving toward the reception desk. "We need to speak with Dr. Pennington, please," she said after showing the frazzled woman her badge.

"He's in with a patient," the woman said. "Might have to take a number."

Whitney glanced around. Nowhere to sit. Hunter was good with crowds, but she didn't need a curious child to pet the big dog. "Can we come into the hallway?"

"Sure." The woman didn't seem to care one way or another. Maybe she and Eddie could compare notes.

The woman buzzed them in since the door stayed locked due to the various medications they kept on hand.

They found two well-worn fabric chairs tucked in a corner and sat down.

"Stay," Whitney ordered Hunter with a brush of her hand across the fur on his head. The big canine settled at her feet. Eddie immediately pulled out his cell and started scrolling while she did a visual scan of the long hallway and wondered if David was here today.

When she heard a scream coming from a room down the hallway, she went on alert. Hunter did the same, lifting his head to her for instructions.

But a nurse came out of the room and shook her head. "Sorry. Patient doesn't like needles."

"Who does?" Eddie said, never taking his eyes off his phone.

Then Whitney looked up and saw Dr. Pennington coming toward them. "What now? I told the receptionist I'm busy."

Whitney stood to greet him. "We have a few more questions. I won't take up much of your time."

The doctor's expression boiled red with anger. "Let's go into my office. I've got patients coming and going. Don't need that dog to bite someone."

Whitney gave Eddie a pointed look, and together they followed the doctor down the hallway to his large office. A bank of windows offered a view of a huge oak tree in the back parking lot.

"If you're going to ask me about the night Veronica was murdered, I told two other officers I was working at the hospital that night."

"You mean the Canyon County Regional Medical Center?" Whitney asked. Dr. Pennington was sometimes on call there, too.

"Of course," Dr. Pennington said. "I was in the ER, and I have witnesses to that. We had a busy night."

"Okay, so we've established that, sir," Whitney said, doing her best to maintain a professional calm. "But...you can help us in another way. Do you know of anyone who might have had beef with Veronica Earnshaw?"

A black SUV pulled up beside Dr. Pennington's foreign sports car in the parking lot. He glanced at the vehicle and started fidgeting. "Look, if you're still wondering who might have killed my ex-wife, go talk to Lloyd Harglow. She left me for him, but that little coupling didn't go very well. She loved his money more than she loved him, and Lloyd doesn't take too well to people who don't fall at his feet."

Whitney had heard Lloyd could be a real pain. But then, so could Veronica. "So you think they could have argued?"

"Argued?" The doctor snorted and started gathering his briefcase and some papers, his gaze moving toward the parking lot again. "They fought all the time. Threatened each other. She'd call me for a shoulder to cry on—not that Veronica ever cried a tear." He scratched his head. "You know, Lloyd's wife hated Veronica, too. For obvious reasons. Veronica didn't care who she stepped on to get what she wanted."

"Okay, we'll speak to both Mr. and Mrs. Harglow again," Whitney said. She was pretty sure they'd both been interviewed, but she'd talk to them if she had to. "Did you and Veronica argue when you were married?"

Dr. Pennington looked affronted. "Like most married couples, yes. Stop fishing for something that isn't there, Officer. We fought, but we always made up."

Whitney wanted to believe him. "Okay. Thanks for your time."

"Glad I could help you." Dr. Pennington glanced around, irritation coloring his features and sarcasm streaming through his words. "Now, if you'll excuse me, I have some business to take care of myself. I have to go."

Whitney glanced at Eddie, but he was busy studying the sports memorabilia on the wall. Useless.

"Thank you, Dr. Pennington," she said. But the doctor was already out in the hallway, barking orders at the nurses. When she nudged Eddie, he seemed to realize the interview was over.

They went out into the hallway, and Whitney looked up to find David conferring with a nurse. "We only have three more patients," he said. "Let's get them taken care of, and you can go home."

David turned and saw Whitney standing in front of Dr. Pennington's office. "Hi," he said, moving toward her. He glanced into the office. "I see he left early again." Then he looked out the window, his gaze turning into a frown.

"Yes." Whitney watched as Eddie went to chat with the receptionist. She hoped he was gathering information. "Does Dr. Pennington do that a lot?"

David nodded, his expression grim as he stared out the window. "According to the nurses, yes. And he left briefly after I got here yesterday. I'm staying late tonight to clear the waiting area."

He glanced back up the hallway and then moved close and pointed toward the window. "Whitney, he got into that dark SUV."

Whitney turned and saw the vehicle peeling out of the back parking area. "Interesting."

"Yes," David said. "Especially since it's almost identical to the one we saw the other day at the train station."

Whitney realized he was right. "I don't know why I didn't catch that myself." Then she shook her head. "But a lot of people around here drive SUVs. This is rugged terrain, and we see all kinds. He took his briefcase with him. Maybe he had a business meeting."

"I could be wrong," David said. "But I'll tell you one thing. I'm going to keep an eye on the doctor. He's good at his job, but why would he come and go like that when we have patients waiting?"

"He doesn't care about the patients," Whitney said. She jotted notes in her pocket pad. "And he doesn't care about Veronica's murder, either."

Tapping her pen against paper, she checked to make sure no one was listening. "He did act a little squirrely today. He couldn't wait to get out of here."

"He keeps to his office most of the time," David said. "And he watches the staff. Doesn't seem to trust anyone. Especially me."

"What do you mean?" Whitney asked. "I'd think he'd appreciate a qualified volunteer."

"He appreciates my work, but my presence seems to irritate him. I focus on the patients. That's mostly what I do." He shrugged and checked his watch. "I don't know. He seems to like to issue veiled threats to anyone who crosses him."

"If he threatens you, you need to let me know."

David's stern expression mirrored what she felt. "Well, he seems to care a lot about something other than this clinic. And I intend to find out what it is."

Whitney put a hand on David's arm. "You need to be careful. He could be dangerous."

David nodded. "We both need to be careful. Something's not right here."

Whitney agreed with him on that, the hair on her neck standing up when she remembered the chief had cautioned them to look for things that seemed off. David had noticed this already, and he'd been here only a few days. She hoped he wouldn't get caught in the middle of any criminal activities. But he'd witnessed two dangerous criminals hauling illegal drugs. He definitely had a target on his back.

NINE

David took a long drink from his bottled water and glanced around the empty clinic. The sun was going down, and he hadn't eaten since this morning's breakfast at the Desert Rose. But it had been a hearty breakfast.

Rosa Helena—Miss Rosa—and her staff cooked up everything from muffins and French toast to omelets and pounds of bacon and sausage. David had eaten some of each since Miss Rosa had kept putting food on his plate. Now he could walk back to the Desert Rose and grab something off the snack table, or maybe he'd try out the Cactus Café. It wasn't far from the clinic, and the nurses had recommended it since it had everything from steak and potatoes to fried chicken and hamburgers.

Besides, he could use a good walk to take his mind off Whitney and the events going on around here. For such a small town, Desert Valley was full of interesting, mysterious people. And apparently a murderer. Did everyone here have secrets?

After checking all of the examining rooms and making sure the trash and laundry had been taken care of and that all the instruments were being properly sterilized, David locked the medicine cabinet and the front door and started out the back. It was kind of amazing that Dr. Pennington had left and returned only to get his car and then leave again. Even more surprising, the rest of the staff members had gladly given David the job of closing up tonight.

David didn't like the lackadaisical way this clinic worked, but he had used the opportunity to explore the entire building for any clues to what the good doctor was up to. Maybe he had a female friend he liked to meet during the day, or maybe he had a family stashed somewhere and he made an appearance now and then. He could have a patient who demanded privacy, so he did what he had to do by sneaking away.

But having been thrown into the middle of some already shady dealings with those drug runners, David's mind was going wild with all sorts of scenarios. He couldn't prove anything, but he could watch and listen. Being in a war zone had honed his senses and his intuition enough that he knew to be cautious.

Had he stepped into a different kind of war zone?

He walked along the row of offices and retail shops that the locals called the Town Center and saw the neon blinking lights of the Cactus Café. He could get something to take back to his room at the Desert Rose, or he could eat at the counter and listen in on the conversations going on around him.

He decided sitting at the counter would be entertaining, and getting the local angle would certainly help him. After he ordered chicken-fried steak and mashed potatoes, he sat back and glanced around. The Cactus Café was decorated appropriately in live cacti of all shapes and sizes, along with murals of the town, including what must have been the first train to come through.

"I hear there's a puppy missing," one old man said to the couple sitting in a booth across from him. "The police know about it. I saw one of them K9 cops talking to several people who live near the training center."

"My wife heard at church the other day that Marian Foxcroft is still in a coma. They got a round-the-clock guard on her hospital room. She donates a lot of those puppies, and when that Earnshaw woman got shot, she offered something like a million dollars to keep all them rookies here to help find the killer. Mighty suspicious that now someone tried to do her in, too. I'm telling you, it ain't safe here anymore."

"And then that whole thing with the train the other day. That poor attendant couldn't wait to go back east after he was released from the hospital. They put a guard on him, too. Drugs moving right under our noses. A lot of good that training center is doing if they can't even find drugs coming through here."

David lowered his head when the waitress brought his food. He didn't want to get into any kind of speculative conversation with the locals. If they recognized him as being the eyewitness, he'd get grilled, but he wouldn't be able to provide any answers. So he kept listening and started piecing together information while he ate his dinner.

But before he'd finished his meal, he realized the incident at the train station could be just the beginning. The drug smugglers might lie low for a while, but they'd be back. They wouldn't want to leave any witnesses behind. Someone had already tried to break into Whitney's house, and that meant Whitney was in a lot of danger, just as he'd figured. Add to that her being involved in investigating a high-profile murder case and the danger became even worse.

Would they keep coming until they hurt her or killed her?

David paid and tipped the waitress and then started walking the short distance back to the Desert Rose. A blue souped-up car driven by a dark-haired man wearing a cowboy hat pulled out of the parking lot. The big motor revved like a growling cat. David eyed the muscle car, thinking he probably should have driven Miss Rosa's decrepit truck to work, but walking was about as quick since the clinic was around the corner from the inn.

When the car moved along Main Street at a slow pace before taking off into the growing darkness, he stared after it, wondering if the man had been following him.

"I'm imagining things," he mumbled. But it didn't hurt to be aware of his surroundings, all things considered.

When he turned the corner, he was surprised to see a patrol car parked in the small front yard of the inn. He hurried up the front steps. "What's going on?"

Whitney turned from the front door. "Miss Rosa called us to report a prowler in the backyard and a blue car idling on the curb."

He glanced inside the house. "I saw that car

headed west on Main Street. But Miss Rosa sees things a lot. She thought a topiary tree was someone's head the other night. And she thinks she's seen your missing puppy. But if I saw that same car, she might be right this time. Where is she now?"

"I'm not sure," Whitney said. "I've knocked and called out." Giving him a firm stare that dared him to move, she said, "Stay here."

"I have a key," David said, fishing it out of his pocket.

She knocked again. "Desert Valley Police, Miss Rosa."

They heard a piercing scream coming from inside the house, followed by a round of gunshots.

TEN

David hurried to slide his key into the lock and opened the big door with a bang. He didn't wait for Whitney.

Whitney ordered Hunter inside, giving the dog a hand signal to search. Drawing her weapon, she hurried through the open stained-glass door. Hunter ran ahead, doing his job like a pro.

Soon angry barks carried throughout the house, coming from the back.

"David?" she called as she cleared the formal sitting room and the elaborate dining room on each side of the long hallway. "David, answer me!"

"Back here."

He sounded winded. Hunter's barks grew more frenzied.

She made it to the big kitchen and then hurried out onto the long sunporch that stretched across the back of the house where she found

David with Miss Rosa. Then another gunshot rang out.

Whitney ducked down and called out, "David, help Miss Rosa."

David knelt beside a Victorian sofa, where Miss Rosa lay with a hand to her head. The petite woman's wiry gray hair stood out like a feather duster against the embroidered pillow behind her. Hunter snarled near the screen door centered on the porch.

Then they heard a car peeling away down the street.

"Is she shot?" Whitney asked, her breath coming fast.

"I'm fine," Miss Rosa said. "I'm short, so he missed. Is someone trying to kill all of us?"

"She saw the shadow again," David explained from behind Whitney, his fingers on Miss Rosa's wrist. "It wasn't the topiary tree, Whitney. She saw a face beyond the sunporch. He came back, but he ran when she screamed."

"A big man," Miss Rosa said through a moan, her dark brown eyes wide open. "I went out to water my rosebushes earlier. I water them every night. You know, they're very hard to grow in this climate, but I make it work. That's when I saw him, right there by the door." She sat up. "I screamed and doused him with the water hose and then I came inside and called 911."

"I'll take Hunter out for a search, but they probably got away when we heard the car leaving," Whitney said. "Do we need to call an ambulance?"

David shook his head. "She's fine. Just scared." He started talking in soothing tones in answer to the innkeeper's many comments and questions. "Yes, I know I'm your only boarder right now. No, I'm not checking out. Yes, I'll watch out for things around here. Let me go get you some water."

"I'm so glad we have a law officer here," Miss Rosa said on a weak note. "I don't abide Peeping Toms or being shot at. Why did he shoot at us?"

"Just rest," David replied. He darted a concerned glance at Whitney before he headed inside to get Miss Rosa's water.

Whitney grabbed her flashlight off her equipment belt and held it over her weapon. Then she opened the screen door. "Go out," she told Hunter. The dog immediately took off toward the back of the long, narrow yard.

Whitney followed and held the flashlight up to the tall white fence, where the fragrant yellow puffballs of an acacia tree hovered like cotton. Nothing there but a tree that covered the fence corner. On the other side, near a rock garden, a blue palm fanned out, rustling in the wind.

Hunter alerted near the gate.

Whitney shined the scant light down to the rocky dirt and saw a red baseball cap by the fence.

Her heart pumped against her rib cage as realization swept through her. Miss Rosa was seeing things all right.

She'd seen a person. And that red baseball cap indicated that the person who'd been near the sunporch door was probably one of the drug smugglers who'd been on the train earlier this week. She'd surprised him, so he'd retaliated by shooting at her.

They were trying to make good on their threats.

The drug runners were hunting down both Whitney and David.

And it would be only a matter of time before they made it all the way inside one of the houses. Whitney shuddered to think what would happen then.

Shelby.

Whitney called Hunter away and whirled to run back to the inn. She had to warn the Carters.

"All is well here, honey," Marilyn said. "We're inside and eating dinner. Jack is here. I'll have him set the alarm."

"Thank you, Marilyn. The cruiser the chief put on our street should be just outside, too."

Gathering her thoughts, Whitney retrieved

her evidence kit from the car so she could bag the red cap. And then she took a quick breath and said a prayer for all of them.

Dear Lord, protect my baby and my friends. God, please protect all of us.

"Are you sure you don't need to go to the ER?"

"Yes." Miss Rosa got up from her chair on the sunporch. "I'm fine. All I did was scream and fall onto a love seat. Now I have to go and check on dinner." She turned at the door to the dining room and slanted her head in a dainty way. "I have a permit, you know. And from now on I can assure you I'll be packing heat."

David watched her head to the kitchen, wishing he hadn't brought this danger into the quaint old inn. "I should go and help her." Then he shook his head. "And I pray she won't make good on that threat. Miss Rosa with a pistol—that's scary."

"We do have drug people out to get us," Whitney said. "She has every right to protect herself."

"So do we," David replied.

The whole place had been checked over for prints and any evidence of a prowler, and the team had combed the woods and yards nearby, looking for bullet fragments and anything else they could find.

Yet they had nothing except the description of the blue car that both David and Miss Rosa had seen, a vintage Camaro that had been over-hauled to get away quickly. That and the red cap, which could offer up some DNA, at least.

Now there was an alert out on that vehicle, too.

"I know, but we can't go into hiding," Whit-ney said. "I have my work, and you volunteer at the clinic. Do you want to hang out at the police station all day?"

"No." Although that would relieve some of his anxieties regarding her.

He glanced out into the dusk to hide his con-cern. But he needed answers to the whole pic-ture since he was knee-deep in this danger. "I know you can't tell me everything, but what's the deal with the missing puppy? And a woman named Marian?"

Her face twisted in surprise. "How do you know about that?"

"The café," he said. "Everyone is talking about the drug couriers and the missing puppy. And Marian being in a coma."

"I can tell you what the public knows. Veron-ica Earnshaw was our master dog trainer. She loved animals and was very good with them.

But she didn't have the best people skills. Shane Weston, one of the rookies, found her dead inside the open gate to the training yard. Gina Perry, another trainer who worked with Veronica, was there with her. At first, people suspected Gina since she and Veronica didn't get along, but she's been cleared. And Shane, too, for that matter."

David held up his hand. "Wait. One of your own was a suspect?"

She nodded. "Briefly. The bullets used to kill Veronica matched those of an antique gun that belonged to Shane's grandfather—a .45 caliber. But thankfully, Shane was cleared since he had a solid alibi."

She stopped and took a breath. "Marian Foxcroft, Ellen's mother, is the woman who funded the department so we could all stay here. She was found unconscious in her home not long after Veronica's death. She's in a coma at the medical center. This case has all of us on edge."

Toying with a rough spot on the arm of the old rocker, she said, "We have briefings almost daily, and we all try to think outside the box."

"No wonder you didn't trust me when you first met me," David said. "You've been dealing with a lot of stuff here and then I pop up, a stranger in town. The Old West is alive and well."

She took a breath and stared out at the grow-

ing night. "It gets worse. Marian donated a lit-
ter of puppies to the training center. Veronica
had been working with them. The night of the
murder, she was at the training center, tagging
them with microchips. When they found Veronica, they realized one of the puppies was missing. Little Marco. Witnesses spotted someone
on a bike picking up the puppy, but it was dark
and the person on the bicycle wore a hoodie,
so the witnesses couldn't tell if it was a man or
woman. We've speculated during our meetings
whether Veronica let the puppy go on purpose.
The evidence from the crime scene points to
that, at least. So we put out flyers all over town,
hoping someone would step up and tell us more
or maybe bring Marco back."

"And you have to follow every lead, just in
case."

She ran a hand over her always neat ponytail.
"We're all assigned to the case, so I've been
making return calls to eliminate some of the
crazy tips that we've received. We need to find
that puppy."

David followed the maze. "The puppy might
help solve the crime?"

"The puppy could be with Veronica's killer,"
Whitney said. "So we have to talk to anyone
who might have seen that puppy. Marco had
been socialized—trained to be around people—

from a very young age. He'd naturally run toward someone, so it's anybody's guess who took him. But yes, the killer might have Marco. Especially if Veronica was letting him go as a message or to give us a clue."

David studied the windows behind them. The inn shimmered with welcoming light. Miss Rosa had turned on all the lamps. "So…did you warn Miss Rosa about all of this?"

Whitney lifted her chin. "Yes, I've talked to her about the missing puppy. She said she saw Marco one night, out in her yard. I checked it out, but I think it was probably the neighbor's calico cat. Kind of the same markings as our missing puppy—fawn colored with a black circle on its head."

David wondered who'd taken the puppy. "This is serious. Me being here put her in danger, too. We've got someone covering up a murder and drug traffickers shooting at us. Any more on those two from the train?"

"No, nothing, but I'm pretty sure one of them was here tonight. I turned the gun over to the property room after we disarmed it. It's been dusted for prints, but it takes a while to hear back from the crime lab in Flagstaff. They'll check it and that scrap of fabric from the pants leg for trace evidence."

"Trace evidence?" David was fascinated, but

mostly, he wanted to keep her here a while longer. He enjoyed talking to her about her work and asking her questions. Her answers gave him hints of her personality. He'd learned to listen to wounded soldiers who needed to talk, so he used that technique on the woman he wanted to get to know better. "You'll have to explain."

"Blood, DNA, hair or fabric fibers."

"And I thought my job was hard."

"We all have hard jobs," she said, getting up. She tilted her head. "Miss Rosa raves to everyone about what a nice young man you are. How you have manners and offer to help her out a lot. She told me you're overhauling her old Chevy pickup."

"I don't know if that jalopy can be overhauled. But she's a sweetheart. She leaves fresh-baked cookies out on the refreshment bar and folds my laundry straight from the dryer." He stared into the house, making sure Miss Rosa was okay. "I'd hate for something to happen to her."

"She's a character," Whitney said. "She has regular boarders passing through, and they don't want to leave. And I'm pretty sure she'd like to keep you as one of them, so stay diligent. This isn't over."

David stood, too, his eyes meeting hers. Funny how he'd just noticed her heart-shaped face. Here in the growing dusk, she looked young and fresh faced, beautiful.

Whitney Godwin was a beautiful woman.

Whoa. In the middle of all of this, he'd still managed to notice? He needed to rein in that notion. Yes, he'd carried her picture near his heart. But he'd done that to honor her brother. Hadn't he? Lucas hadn't sent him here to make the moves on his sister. David would have to tamp down any attraction he might be feeling. They both needed to be aware of their surroundings, not each other.

He leaned down. "You don't need to worry about me."

Whitney tossed her ponytail and stared out across the salmon-colored roses blooming along the porch railing. "I can't seem to *stop* worrying about you."

"I can take care of myself."

"I don't doubt that but…this situation is growing more and more dangerous." Then she turned stoic again. "Now we need to search for a blue car."

"It took off in a hurry. Must have dropped off the shooter and doubled back."

He didn't want her to leave, but he figured Shelby was waiting. She'd be anxious to get home to her little girl. The image of Whitney holding that cute little baby invaded his efforts to ignore his growing attraction to her.

And before he could stop them, the words were out of his mouth. "Hey, maybe we could get together later in the week," he called as she headed down the steps. "Dinner or something. Low-key, and we'll be careful."

Whitney stopped by her car, surprise chasing confusion in her expression. "Maybe, yeah, sure. Maybe this weekend. If the chief doesn't put me in protective custody."

"If he does, I'm going in there with you," David blurted. "You can't leave me out here alone. We're a team now, right?"

"I'd never leave you alone," she replied.

Then they stopped talking and stared at each other. "We can make jokes but…this is no laughing matter," she said. "I wasn't too scared before, but now…I'm terrified. For Shelby, for Miss Rosa and for you, David."

David wanted to hold her and assure her that he'd take care of this, but…he had no idea how to do that.

Another long day.

Glad to be home, Whitney checked on Shelby for the fourth time. Her baby was sleeping, the little lamb night-light showing her cherubic face in muted white and yellow. After the scare at the inn last night, she'd explained to Marilyn and Jack that they needed to be cautious, too.

"I don't think they'll try anything with you but… I just want you to be aware. Keep Shelby in for a while."

"I will," Marilyn had said. "We won't go for our afternoon strolls until you think it's safe."

Marilyn and Jack knew the danger involved in Whitney's work, but they seemed to take it in stride. Jack's garage was only five minutes away, so he'd reassured her he could be home very quickly if need be. Marilyn had taken self-defense classes years ago when Jack worked at night, and they had a good alarm system. She didn't seem afraid, but she wasn't someone who'd be careless or take too many risks, either.

Now Whitney went back over her week. She'd tracked down false leads and filed numerous reports. But she kept returning to the conversations she'd had with two possible witnesses early this morning before she'd gone to work.

"I saw that puppy," the woman had told her through a screen door, her hair still in sponge curlers. "He was running down Desert Valley Road all by his lonesome. Cute little thing, too. I almost stopped and picked him up, but when I looked back, I didn't see him."

"Describe him," Whitney said.

"Tan colored with a black blob on his little face. As if he fell into some chocolate."

Marco.

One other witness, a scrawny skateboarder, had told her he'd also seen Marco. "But somebody on a bike picked him up, so I thought he belonged to the rider."

The kid had verified what they already knew.

"I saw someone with the puppy," the kid had said, his foot flipping his worn skateboard up and into his hands. "I mean, it was kinda dark and whoever it was had on a hoodie that covered their head and face. But I do know they took that puppy and rode away on that bike."

Both the kid and the older woman who'd talked to her had told Whitney they had hoped someone would take the puppy to a shelter or maybe turn it in to the police.

But that hadn't happened. And nothing else was standing out. No word from the lab in Flagstaff on the drug couriers and nothing substantial regarding Veronica's murder. Whitney kept wondering if the two were random incidents or if they might possibly be connected.

At their briefing this morning, Whitney gave the report on the two witnesses who'd seen someone take Marco, and then she reported her findings after talking to Dr. Pennington. She mentioned Lloyd Harglow.

"Dr. Pennington says Lloyd and Veronica fought a lot. She confided in him, apparently. He implicated Harglow as a possible suspect."

James Harrison, one of the rookie K9 officers, looked over at her, his blue eyes full of skepticism. "I interviewed Lloyd Harglow on Monday after the murder. He was at a meeting with city officials on the night Veronica died. After the meeting, three of them went out for a late dinner in Canyon County City. I have several witnesses who corroborated his story." James pushed at his spiked blond hair. "He did admit that their fling went sour after a few months, but he insists he'd never hurt Veronica. He's trying to patch things up with his wife, who has an alibi, too, by the way."

The chief moved on to Whitney and David's run-in with the couriers. "What do you have on the drug runners, Godwin?"

Whitney went back over the occurrences at her house and at the inn. "The drug couriers are trying to scare us. Mr. Gallagher is safe since he doesn't live here but…I did see their faces, and so did the one other eyewitness. The shooter fired two shots and then left," she said, almost thinking out loud.

"But?" Chief Jones pinned her with his stark gaze. "You look as if you have something else on your mind."

Whitney cleared her throat. "Drug runners usually follow through pretty quickly. They wouldn't waste time walking around just to scare someone. Frankly, I'm surprised they didn't get into a shootout with me." Then she glanced at her friends. "I have a baby to consider, sir."

"And I don't have the manpower to guard everyone," the chief replied. "You do what you need to keep little Shelby safe."

"Yes, sir."

"They'll keep comin'," Officer Ryder Hayes said. Like James, he had the blond hair and blue eyes that seemed to make some women swoon. Good-looking but guarded, Ryder was still mourning the unsolved death of his wife five years ago. Melanie had been robbed and murdered the night of the police dance. She'd never made it to the party.

Mike Riverton had died from a fall on the stairs of his home on the night of the dance two years ago.

Brian had died in a house fire on that same night last year.

A clear pattern, but one they couldn't figure out. The night of the annual police dance was significant, but how? And why?

"Whitney?"

She looked up to see Ryder and the others

waiting for her to respond. "Yes. Drug runners are usually brutal and swift. So far, we've managed to scare them away, and based on the cap we found at the inn, we can assume that was the drug runners." Then she added, "But I wonder if the prowler in my yard could be related to Veronica's murder and not the drug runners. What if someone thinks I know something or have something they want?"

"We've had a lot of reports about people doing that recently," Ellen Foxcroft said. "Snooping, but they don't take anything. Maybe these intruders are just random. Kids out for fun."

"Or the drug runners could be casing places, hoping to find any opportunity," James pointed out. "You got to them and scared them off before they could get to you."

"That could be it." They could easily have killed Hunter and her and possibly David, too. Something didn't make sense, but she had too much on her mind to piece it together. "In any case, I'll be vigilant, and I've warned David Evans to do the same."

"Do you trust him?" Ryder asked. "I mean, he's new in town, and he happened to be on the same train as those alleged couriers."

She answered without even thinking about it. "I do trust David. He's not involved with the drug couriers. He put his life on the line to help Mr. Gallagher."

Since she'd already reported on his background check coming back clean, she didn't offer any further explanations. But she hadn't told anyone why David was here. She didn't want anyone to think his presence was impacting her work.

Even if it was beginning to do just that.

She'd have to be careful about her feelings toward David. She'd already had one impulsive love affair, and she was pretty sure everyone around here had figured that out. She couldn't afford to mess up her personal life again, so she'd have to keep her comments on a professional level. And her feelings, too.

Just before she left for the day, the department secretary, Carrie, came by her desk. "Hey, the chief needs you in his office, Whitney. He doesn't look happy," she added nervously.

"Okay." Whitney followed Carrie down the hallway.

"Hope you're not in trouble," Carrie said, her brown eyes sympathetic.

Whitney stood near the open door, hoping the same thing. "Sir, you wanted to see me?"

"Shut the door, Godwin."

Whitney braced herself and took a calming breath.

"Have a seat."

"Sir, what is it?"

"You remember coming to me about the rookie deaths and suggesting how they didn't seem so random to you? You were concerned because of the way they each died, especially Brian Miller."

She nodded, but before she could respond, he kept on talking. "And since Marian Foxcroft made her demands and then threw in her generous offer, I've had all of you going back over files and trying to pinpoint something to connect all of this."

"Yes, sir," she said. "But it's only been a few weeks. We've all been taking turns with the case files. I know Mrs. Foxcroft wanted these cases declared accidents, but…"

"But some of you seem to think differently. Especially you."

"How could I not?" she asked. "The two rookies' backgrounds don't match up with the way they both died. Mike was an expert mountain climber, and yet he died from a fall down the stairs. And Brian's whole family died from a horrible house fire. He would never light a candle in his home, let alone leave it unattended. But that's what the fire marshal thinks happened."

"Yeah, well, the police dance is coming up

again," Chief Jones said. "I'm not saying I agree or disagree with your theory, but yes, there does seem to be a certain pattern, especially with Melanie Hayes's murder and the rookies' deaths all happening on the night of prior dances. And even though Marian wanted the rookies' deaths ruled as accidents, she's not the chief of police. I am, and I don't want another murder on my hands. If she ever wakes up, I'll convince her of that. I want you to investigate that angle. Talk to anyone who knew them." He leaned his head down then cast his gaze back up to her. "Can you handle that? And don't leave out Melanie Hayes."

"Melanie? So you agree the same person might have killed Melanie?"

"What did I just say, Godwin?"

"Yes, sir. Go over her case, too." Whitney would handle it. She'd been trying to get to the bottom of this for a long time, but she'd tried to be careful since she wasn't sure who to trust. She'd talked about Brian's death with Gina Perry a couple of weeks ago. No one here knew for sure that Brian was Shelby's father, but she was fairly certain Gina had guessed. Now, at least, she had the chief on her side, even if he didn't know the whole story regarding Brian and her. "I'll get right on it."

When she left the chief's office, Carrie gave

her the thumbs-up sign. Had she heard the chief's loud voice? It didn't matter. Everyone who worked at the station wanted those deaths solved.

Now, home at last and clean from her shower, she'd just settled down in her pj's to catch up on the evening news when her cell buzzed. The caller ID showed the name David Evans.

She almost didn't answer. David was too tempting, and she had to stay centered and focused right now. She'd also need to tell him the truth about Brian.

"Hi," she said. Muting the television, she curled her legs up onto the couch. Hunter was in the hallway by Shelby's room. On guard for the night.

"Hi. I got Miss Rosa settled down last night. And I made sure the security lights are all working. This old inn could use a security system, but she says she doesn't have the money for that. Or a good hot water heater, either, apparently."

"No hot water? How's that working for you?"

"Let's just say I come clean pretty quickly these days."

She grinned at that. "Should I send a patrol around, just in case?"

"To fix the water heater or to watch the inn?"

She enjoyed his sense of humor. "They could

probably do both. Small towns tend to have multitaskers by necessity."

"Miss Rosa would probably feel better with a patrol car in the area," he said. "But I'll be okay. You have enough to deal with right now."

"I'm trained to take care of such things."

"I know. Talk about threatening my manhood."

"So you don't like it when a woman comes to your rescue?"

"Oh, I don't mind at all, but…I've never had the tables turned on me. Takes getting used to, I reckon."

"Maybe Lucas sent you here for that very reason."

"He was tricky, your big brother. He loved to play practical jokes on the whole platoon."

"That sounds like Lucas. Always joking around." She stopped smiling and bit back tears. "I miss him every day."

"I know. He was the best of the best."

"I'm so glad that you're here, David. And that you knew Lucas."

"So you wouldn't mind if your big brother had an ulterior motive?"

She couldn't lie about that. Lucas might have handpicked David for her, but she couldn't go beyond friendship with him right now.

"I didn't like you being here at first, but…it's almost as if he sent me one last gift."

"That's a nice way to look at it."

"It's good to talk about him with someone who was with him on a daily basis. No one here knew him, so they all draw a blank when I mention him."

"They don't know what to say. Death is a tough topic."

"Yes. Yes, it is." She wanted to tell him about Brian, but not tonight. She planned to pull all the files on Brian's death, along with those of Mike Riverton and Melanie Hayes, first thing tomorrow. But for now, she could use a little distraction.

So they talked about random things well into the night, laughing and discussing everything from movies to ice cream to the Arizona weather.

And when her head finally hit the pillow, she thought of what it would be like to have a man like David in her life for longer than a few weeks.

ELEVEN

Friday, David knocked on Whitney's front door and waited. They'd agreed to go out to dinner tonight, but Whitney had decided they should stay in.

"I'm afraid to take Shelby out of the house." Two days had passed with no incidents, but that didn't mean they were safe. If it made her feel better to have her baby in her sights right now, he certainly understood. He also figured the baby would serve as a buffer to keep him from getting too close.

She opened the door with a smile playing across her lips. A smile that left him speechless. She looked amazing in a casual denim sundress and strappy sandals, her blond hair falling around her face.

In her uniform, she was impressive.

In a dress, she was a knockout.

"Come in," she said waving him in with her hand in the air. "I ordered delivery from the steak house. It should be here in fifteen minutes. Have a seat, and I'll go get Shelby."

"Okay." He followed her inside and patted Hunter's head, sensing that she still wasn't sure about this date. "Hey, big boy. How you doing?"

Hunter enjoyed being scratched between the ears.

"He's looking forward to a night of rest," Whitney said. "And so am I."

David sat down on the blue chair, Hunter at his feet. "Long week, huh?"

"Yes. And today was the longest. I've been pulling files all day, hoping to find clues."

That explained things. She was exhausted and probably preoccupied with watching her back. Better that they stayed here, even if it did mean things would be more intimate.

Whitney came back into the living room, little Shelby in her arms. The baby shot a smile toward David, but he was pretty sure Shelby was really smiling at her buddy Hunter. The dog seemed to have a special bond with the baby.

"Need any help?"

She sat down and stretched some bright green baby socks that mimicked real shoes over Shelby's kicking feet. "No. By the way, Chief Jones pulled me aside yesterday and told me to do some asking around regarding a few cold cases."

"That sounds dangerous."

"Not really. A lot of what we do involves pounding the pavement and asking the right questions. It's the boring part of our job, but it's still the best way to follow through on leads."

David watched her with her baby and wished she'd chosen another profession. No wonder Lucas worried about her. But it wasn't David's place to protest Whitney's work. She was more than capable of doing her job.

And yet, he also pictured this same image in a different frame that included him coming home after a long day to kiss his wife and baby.

Whoa. He needed to clear that image right out of his head. Whitney wasn't his wife, and Shelby wasn't his daughter.

"Just be careful," he said to hide the awareness racing throughout his system.

Whitney finished gathering Shelby's things. "I will. Routine stuff." Then she did a little pivot. "I'm still missing her other white bootie. The dryer seems to eat them."

"Well, she looks great," David said, watching as she put Shelby into her play swing. "A well-dressed little girl." Then he looked at Whitney. "And her mother is a well-dressed woman."

Whitney's smile widened as something like heat lightning sizzled between them.

After they settled on the couch and started munching on chips and salsa, she turned to

David. "I need you to know the truth, David. The chief finally gave me permission to pursue something I've had on my mind for a while now. I'm working on my own time tomorrow to find out what really happened to Brian Miller."

David saw the shadows falling across her face. "Who's that?"

"One of the rookies from last year's class. He died in a house fire last summer, on the night of the police dance. It's a fund-raising event we hold every year. I believe someone murdered him. I've always believed that, along with a couple of others. Now the chief thinks so, too."

David let that soak in. "Okay. Does this have anything to do with the dog trainer's murder?"

"It could," she said. "We need to establish some sort of connection between all the deaths with the K9 Training Center in common—the two K9 rookies, Melanie Hayes, who was the wife of a then rookie, and the lead dog trainer."

David could understand that. "Makes sense."

Whitney glanced at Shelby and then looked straight into David's eyes. "I have another important reason to investigate Brian's death," she said. "He's the father of my baby."

David stared back in shock, thinking that now a whole lot of other things were beginning to make sense, too.

"So you had a thing for a fellow rookie?"

"We weren't rookies yet," she corrected him. "We went through training together." She kept checking on Shelby. The baby kicked her chubby legs. "But it was more than just a thing to me. I thought… Well, never mind what I thought. It didn't work out."

David could see it all now. "Did he know about your pregnancy before he died?"

She shook her head. "No. Brian lived in a house in another town about twenty miles from here. He worked part-time as a security guard at a strip mall near his house, so he stayed there most of the time, even when he was training at the center with the rest of us."

She closed her eyes. "I fell for him right away. I was naive, and I hadn't had a serious boyfriend since high school. Brian made it so easy."

Shelby started fussing, her little feet gearing up for a tantrum.

"She's getting hungry," Whitney said. "I can go ahead and feed her, since our food isn't here yet."

David lifted Shelby up out of her little playpen. "And we can finish this conversation while you're at it."

Whitney wished she hadn't just blurted it out, but she had to tell David sometime. Better tonight, before she got involved in searching for answers. Tonight they could have a few quiet hours. Tomorrow she'd get serious about these deaths.

Whitney put Shelby in her high chair and offered her a cracker while she prepared the tiny jar of baby food. "We weren't supposed to fraternize. But going over to his house for pizza and movies didn't seem like fraternizing. It felt so natural, so right. We became an item even though we tried to keep it a secret. I thought I'd found the one, at last."

"But it didn't turn out that way?"

"No." She wished she could sugarcoat it, but Shelby was living proof of how far Brian and she had taken things. "We were halfway through training when I realized I might be pregnant. I did a home pregnancy test, got tested at our clinic here and followed up with a doctor in another town, just to be sure and to set up health care for my baby. When I got a positive confirmation, I immediately went to Brian's house to tell him. And found him with another woman."

David's frown clouded with anger. "What?"

"Yes. Kissing her and telling her pretty much all the same things he'd been telling me. I saw them and heard all of it through the open window by the front door." She smiled while she spooned carrots and peas into Shelby's little mouth. "I left before he saw me through the window. The police dance was the next week-end. We were supposed to meet up there, and I thought maybe if I told him he was going to be a father, he'd…change."

She blinked back the tears that always stayed right below the surface, the tears she refused to shed. "But he never made it to the dance. His house burned down that night."

David stayed quiet for a couple of minutes, but Whitney could tell he was doing the math in his head. "So you decided not to complete the training?"

"How could I?" she said after she'd finished feeding Shelby. "It was too risky, and besides, I'm pretty sure I would have gotten kicked out anyway." She shrugged. "I had a little money saved up from the job I left in Tucson to become a police officer. I went back to work for the insurance company until I had Shelby."

"So you had a job, health insurance and a place to stay in Tucson. Shelby was born there?"

"Yes." Wiping at Shelby's dimpled face, she tried to explain. "Once I was settled there, I planned to tell my brother. But I kept putting it off. And then, of course, I got the news that he'd been wounded and had died." Putting her elbows on the table, Whitney knuckled her hands against her chin. "I wish I'd told him. He would have been angry and worried, but Lucas would have loved being an uncle."

David finally looked up and into her eyes. "Yes, Lucas would have loved Shelby."

"I've made a mess of so many things," Whitney said. "But I thank God every day for Shelby and for the lessons I've learned. I'm trying to be a good mother to her. I won't be so naive next time, though."

And she needed to remember that pledge each time her feelings for David made her become all mushy and hopeful. Shelby was her first priority now. She had to guard her heart and take care of her little girl.

He gave her a wry smile, followed by a serious look of appraisal. "And yet you're determined to prove that her father was murdered."

"Yes," she said. "Brian might not have been the best choice as a boyfriend but…he would have been a good police officer. And I'd like to believe that whether he loved me or not, he would have been a good father to Shelby. He can't have that chance now, but I can find out who took his life."

"And what if that person comes looking for you, too, Whitney? What happens then?"

She hadn't thought about that, but it wouldn't stop her. "I don't intend on letting that happen," she replied. "Everyone is so caught up in Veronica's murder that I don't think I'll have to worry about them noticing anything different."

She didn't tell him that she'd already pored over Melanie Hayes' file, gone back to the houses near the Hayes ranch and questioned neighbors. But the only thing she'd found out was from a widow who said Melanie often took that path home since she loved to walk for exercise.

That could mean someone had been watching her or knew her well enough to be aware of her habits.

"Unless these deaths are connected to Veronica's death," David said, bringing Whitney back to the present. "You said yourself the same person might have committed all of these murders."

She knew she shouldn't tell him anything more, but she wanted to be honest. "Chief Jones has finally given me the go-ahead to do some more digging. Brian knew a lot of people, and he probably left a few broken hearts in his wake. I need to find out who might have had it in for him, because I know this was no accident. Even if I didn't want to do this, which I do, the chief put me on this case."

"Yes, since you've made it known how you feel."

"The other rookies are beginning to agree with me." She watched as Shelby's eyelids started drooping. "Shouldn't I let him know my suspicions, especially if we all have concerns?"

"Yes. I can't argue with that. You're a good cop. You were right to go to your superior with this."

"Well, everyone pretty much feels the same now that we've been comparing notes," she said. "None of it makes any sense if the deaths aren't connected."

"No, it doesn't. I get why you're so determined," he said. "You're also investigating this on your own time. Are you obsessed with this because you couldn't save Brian?"

"Yes, I am," she admitted. "I'm obsessed with finding out the truth." She lifted Shelby out of her little chair and held her tight. "I can't seem to find any closure. I'll always wonder if he might have been a good father to Shelby, even if he clearly didn't love me."

David jabbed a chip into the spicy dip. "It won't bring him back."

"No, but it will bring about justice. That's all I have left to show my daughter what real honesty and integrity are all about."

"I can see why you'd want that. So no problem. I mean, you don't need my permission anyway."

But she wanted his approval for some reason. His opinion mattered to her, even if she'd only known him for a week. Reminding herself not to rush into anything, she took a deep breath. Holding Shelby, she glanced at the clock in the kitchen.

"The food is late. I'm sorry."

David stood up and turned to stare into the empty fireplace.

"We won't be able to hang out as much," she told him. "Maybe you should leave and get on with your life."

"I am getting on with my life," he said, pivoting to face her. "But I'm not leaving Desert Valley yet."

"I just told you—"

"I know. You'll be busy." He leaned in, his tone even and firm. "But you won't be alone. I'm going to help you find out the truth, whether you like having me around or not."

Before she could protest, the doorbell rang. Whitney grabbed some cash and hurried to answer it. David took the baby so she could pay the delivery person and take the food.

When the door opened, Whitney was surprised but handed the skinny blond-haired man the money. "Thank you. Keep the change."

The man moved into the room and handed Whitney the big bag full of food. "You two have the cutest little girl."

That innocent comment did not go over well.

Whitney's eyes crashed with David's, embarrassment and awareness hitting her in the gut. "Uh...she's mine. David is just a friend."

The scrawny man watched as Whitney took the food and set it on the nearby table. Then he stepped back and drew a pistol out from underneath his lightweight jacket. "Too bad."

TWELVE

"Shelby," Whitney cried, one hand reaching for her baby.

"Watch it," the man said, the gun aimed at David and Shelby. "Don't make any moves, lady."

In the hallway, Hunter stood and growled.

"Call off the dog. Now," the man said as he walked around the room, his beady eyes darting here and there.

David gave Whitney a warning glance. He knew where she kept her gun, and there was no way she'd be able to get to it.

Hunter started barking, and then everything happened so fast, David could only react, his mind racing back to the many times he'd had to take cover.

Whitney shouted to Hunter to attack. Then she head butted the man wielding the gun, her hand going up to grab his arm. She wrestled with him, the weapon caught between them as she slammed him back against the wall next to the front door.

"Hold her," Whitney shouted to David as Hunter came charging up the hallway. "Get Shelby out of here."

David wasn't about to leave Whitney, but he had to protect the now frightened little girl. Taking the sobbing baby, he dived behind the couch and watched as Hunter attacked the man who was wrestling with Whitney.

The man screamed in pain, the gun went off and then the man slumped against the wall, with Hunter still biting into his leg with a vengeance.

Whitney rolled away, the man's weapon in her hand. David lifted up, his hand over Shelby's head as he ran toward Whitney.

"No," Whitney said. "I've got this. Take her to the bedroom and calm her down." The fear in her blue eyes floored David. "Please, David."

David couldn't speak so he hurried to the nursery. He tried to soothe Shelby. Finding her pacifier, he sat down in the big rocking chair by the baby's bed and rocked her until her sobs subsided. He didn't know if he could ever let her go again.

While he sat, he listened to sirens and dogs and voices shouting over each other. He knew what was going on. Whitney was being questioned and checked over. She'd killed a man right here in her house. And he'd seen the whole thing.

At least he'd shielded Shelby from the worst of it.

"It's okay," he said to the sleepy, tired little girl. "It's okay. I won't let anything happen to you or your mother, I promise."

But even as he made that vow, he wondered how in the world any of them would survive this.

Whitney's heart was beating so fast, she felt dizzy. How could she have been so careless as to put Shelby in danger?

Just another reason why she needed to stay away from David. He made her forget her responsibilities and her duty as a mother. But dccp inside, she knew this wasn't David's fault.

Someone wanted her dead. And it was anyone's guess about who that someone might be. Drug runners or Veronica's killer or both? Had she stirred up too much attention by asking too many questions?

Now she moved down the short hallway to Shelby's room, needing to see her daughter, to touch her, to hold her.

"David?"

"We're good," he said from the rocking chair.

Whitney stopped in the doorway. He held

Shelby against his broad chest as if she were the most precious thing in the world.

She heard Shelby sniffle in her sleep and felt her heart crush against her rib cage. *Dear God, protect my baby and David. Help me to keep us safe, Lord.*

"David...I..."

"Breathe," David said. "Slow, deep breaths."

She did as he told her, the doorjamb steadying her. "Shelby?"

"Shelby is just fine. She's got her pacifier and she's fast asleep. I think she likes my singing."

"That's my girl," Whitney said, tears pricking at her eyes.

For as long as she lived, she'd never forget this tender scene. This man who'd fought so hard to get to her had taken care of her baby while she'd done what she had to do.

For once, he'd listened to her.

But this scene made him more of a hero than any shootout ever could. At least in her eyes anyway.

She lifted off the wall and hurried to sink down beside the rocking chair. Kissing Shelby, she glanced up and into David's brown eyes. "Thank you."

His gaze held hers. He started to speak, but the sound of boots hitting the hallway floor pulled her away.

"Godwin?"

"In here," she called, standing and wiping her eyes.

David gave her a nod. "We're okay here."

Rookie K9 officer Shane Weston stepped into the doorway, his partner, Bella, by his side. "Hey, you okay?"

The tall, dark-haired cop's expression was hard to read. His gaze moved to where David sat rocking the baby.

"Yes," Whitney said to the question in his green eyes. "David and I were going to have dinner. I thought we'd be safe here."

She gave David an appreciative glance. "David...took care of Shelby for me."

Shane looked at David with a new respect. "Okay, the ME has taken the body away. No ID yet, but we'll know something soon." He shuffled in his boots. "We found the real delivery person knocked out in the bushes by the front door. I guess our man dragged him in there before the cruiser watching your house noticed, took the food and came on in."

"I had alerted the officer that I was having food delivered, so don't blame him. Is the deliveryman okay?"

"Yeah. Probably a concussion. He said he didn't see who did it. Kid's pretty shaken."

"It has to be the drug runners. They're watching," Whitney said. "They knew we were here and they waited for an opportunity. Seeing a delivery person walking up to the door gave them an easy way inside."

"Yep. But they might have come in later, when you were alone," Shane pointed out. "Good thing you had some help."

Whitney eyed David. "Yes. I'm thankful for that."

"We knew it would only be a matter of time," David said. "They came for me the other night, and now they're following us."

Shane stepped back. "Do you want me to put a stronger detail on your house, Whitney?"

"No," she said at the same time David said, "Yes."

"No? Yes?" Shane looked amused. "Which do I listen to?"

"I'll watch out for her," David said, lifting from the chair to hand Shelby to Whitney. "Whitney's brother, Lucas, and I served together in Afghanistan. And I came here because he was concerned about her before he died. I can watch out for her."

"You don't have to do that," Whitney said. "I can take care of myself. The department is stretched as it is. I don't need a heavy detail trailing around with me."

David studied Shane, probably figuring he'd

protest, but Shane just stood there like a solid wall, a knowing gleam in his eyes.

"Yeah, I heard rumors that you'd come all this way to see Godwin," Shane finally said. "But that doesn't mean you can protect her. You're both in danger."

"I'll set up camp in her backyard if I have to," David said. Then he planted his feet apart and crossed his arms over his chest. "Because like I've already told Whitney, I'm not leaving any time soon."

"I told you, you can't stay in my house."

Whitney stared over at David while she fed Shelby a bottle before putting her back to bed. Her little girl was exhausted, and so was she. She was almost too tired to argue with David.

Everyone else had left. A different patrol car sat outside, relieving the officer who'd somehow missed the delivery kid being knocked out cold in her yard. But she still couldn't blame the tired patrolman. These people were sneaky and trained in finding their way into any situation.

"I can't let you go through this alone," David said, his eyes reminding her of rocks at dusk, so dark and mysterious, hard-edged. "Not after tonight."

"What part of 'I'm a police officer' don't

you get?" she asked, knowing he should leave. Wishing she could let him sleep on her couch.

No. She had to get that kind of notion right out of her head. Still vulnerable from Brian's deception and death and still all warm and fuzzy from the way David had protected Shelby earlier, she had no business thinking any kind of warm thoughts about the man standing at her kitchen counter. They barely knew each other, but it felt as if they'd known each other always.

David gave her an appreciative glance. "I've seen you in action. But... I know what evil people can do, Whitney. It's dangerous." He pointed to the crime scene tape stretched across the front door. "That hit man forced his way into your house. We've messed in their world, and now they'll keep coming until they eliminate us. And they can do that in awful, torturous ways."

"Are you trying to scare me?"

"Yes," he said. Stalking around the counter, he set down the bottle of water she'd given him. "I can't help but worry about you and Shelby. You both could have been killed tonight."

Whitney knew he was right. And she was so weary. So very weary. "I'm going to check on her one more time."

David picked up a picture of Shelby. "She's beautiful," he said on a strained whisper.

"I know." Whitney peeked out the windows

and turned the volume up high on the baby monitor. Hunter followed her around the house, still on high alert. The chief had let her stay here tonight only because of Shelby and...probably because David was here. Chief Jones had also stationed James Harrison and his partner, Hawk, out in the backyard.

She should have felt safe. And yet she shivered.

"Stay," she said to Hunter after she'd kissed Shelby and tugged her blanket over her. His trusting, dark-eyed gaze moved from her to Shelby's bed. Hunter circled and lay down between the door and the bed. "Guard," Whitney said.

Hunter would attack anyone who tried to come into this room. She knew that, but she couldn't stop the shiver that curled around her like a rattlesnake.

Checking the shadows one more time, Whitney planned her own attack on the man waiting in the den. She had to make David see that he didn't have to be her protector.

And yet something deep inside her heart loved how he'd rushed to her defense again by insisting he'd take care of her. Had she ever had anyone fight so much for her and with her?

Not in this way, no. Her brother had been her knight in shining armor, but Lucas had gone off to the other side of the world, fighting an even bigger battle. She'd accepted that and moved on with her goals and dreams, hoping to make him proud.

Then Brian had come along, and she'd placed such high hopes in what she believed to be their love. But that had been only a daydream, a false assumption based on her misguided illusions.

She wouldn't make that mistake again so soon after being burned, even if it seemed her brother had practically handpicked the man who'd come here. David needed to leave Desert Valley and move on to whatever his future held. Now to convince him of that. And maybe herself, too.

But when she walked into the den and saw him folding a baby blanket, her heart did a little heated dance of joy.

Wrong man, but right moves. He'd make a good husband and daddy for some lucky woman. "You're exhausted," she said, an edge of exhaustion hiding the tremors cresting in her body.

"Yes," he said, turning to stare at her. "But I can't leave you alone here."

She sank down on the couch, fatigue weighing on her like a suffocating dry heat while she tried not to look at the chalk lines on the floor where the intruder's body had fallen. "I've been on my own for a long time now."

"I admire that about you," he said, sitting down beside her with one booted foot resting across the knee of his other leg.

He took up too much space. On her couch. In her house. Inside her head. Maybe if she just talked to him. "You've been on your own a while, too."

"Yes. And I don't like being told what to do. I don't like asking for help, either." He shrugged. "What do you want me to do? Just leave? I can't. I'd never forgive myself."

"And why do you need to stay?" she asked, grabbing a pillow to hold so she wouldn't be tempted to touch him. "You don't owe me anything, David. And this obligation you feel toward my brother is noble but unnecessary."

David turned to her, his dark gaze roaming over her with a look of awareness that left her emotionally stripped. "What if it's not about Lucas anymore?" he asked, one finger moving to touch her arm. "What if I want to stick around for you and Shelby?"

Whitney shot up off the couch. "No." She shook her head and tried to ignore the tingle of anticipation David's touch had ignited. "No, that is not such a good idea."

"Why?" he asked, not moving. But his gaze on her, searching, questioning, told her just how dangerous being around him had become.

"You know why. I'm a single mother. An unmarried mother who had my baby alone. No one here knows the truth, but I think some of them suspect. I mean, Brian and I flirted a lot, and it's a small town. I'm sure they know, but…no one's condemned me yet. I'm working hard to prove myself. I have to. Brian and I weren't supposed to be together in the first place, so I guess I'm still trying to protect him, too."

David stood and then moved close to where she paced in front of the empty fireplace. "What's all of that got to do with you and me?"

"Everything," Whitney said, inching away from him. "I have to put Shelby first. I need to help solve this murder case and…I want to find out the truth about Brian's death." She shrugged and crossed her arms over her midsection. "I need to stay focused on my continued training and my job or I could ruin my entire future as a K9 officer."

He shook his head. "I understand your work is important, but it's dangerous, looking for drug smugglers and a killer. Let someone else handle some of those investigations."

"No, because it's *part* of my work, and it will help me to understand…why Brian had to die that way. I have to know."

"Will knowing change anything?"

"I don't know," she said, anger tamping down

the attraction she'd tried so hard to ignore. "Nothing can change this tragedy, but at least I'd feel as if I found justice and the truth. Brian might not have been the man I wanted him to be, but he didn't have to die in such a horrible way, either. I want the truth, and I want whoever did this to suffer the consequences."

Something shifted in David's eyes. His expression hardened into an unyielding acceptance. "You're not over him, are you?"

Whitney's breath went shallow while her pulse leaped. "I have to solve the mystery behind his death. Otherwise, how can I put Brian behind me when I see him each time I look at my little girl?"

David backed away, nodding as he moved to the couch. "Okay, so you're not ready for anything heavy right now. I get that. But…I'm here, and I'm staying until I at least know you'll be safe."

"You can't stay here with…me," she said, relief washing over the regret she already felt. "I've changed since Shelby was born. I'm trying to be a better example, for her sake."

It would be so easy to let him into her life, to invite him to stay here with her and Shelby. But she couldn't do that. She'd turned her life around, and she'd made a pledge to stay smart and in control for her baby and for her own redemption.

"I won't," he finally said. "I'll stay at the Desert Rose but…I'm going to help you with this investigation."

"How do you plan on doing that?" she asked, amazed that he refused to give up. "You're not qualified."

"I'll watch Shelby for you or go with you to some of the places you'll want to check out, and I'll wait in the car or outside. Kind of a bodyguard. I'm good at observing situations. I had to be since I dealt with a lot of things at once during the heat of battle."

"Is that what kept you alive? Being watchful and alert?"

"I don't know what kept me alive but…I intend to live my life to the fullest, with a strong faith that I'm here for a reason. I believe we all have a purpose in life."

Whitney wished her faith could be that sure and solid. "I believe that, too, but I can't have it on my conscience if something happens to you, David."

"And I can't walk away," he said, moving toward her again. "Not now. We're both up to our eyeballs in this. I'm an eyewitness to a possible drug smuggling operation. I was threatened at gunpoint. If we work together, we might solve this thing a lot sooner. And if, after we do find the smugglers or your killer, you still want me to leave, then I will."

Whitney decided she didn't have want to argue with him. "All right," she said, wondering if she'd regret this. "But you can't get in my way, or try to protect me, or tackle any bad guys. Let me do what I'm trained to do, okay?"

"Okay. Unless someone is trying to harm you," he said. "Then…I'll do whatever it takes—"

"David."

"As a last resort," he finished, a soft, sure smile lifting his lips. "Deal?" He reached out a hand as if to shake hers.

"Deal," she said. "I could use some neutral eyes to help me go over the particulars. But you can only tag along when I'm on my own time. You can't be part of an active investigation."

"I'll tag along whenever I can," he said, his eyes holding hers. "And you'll have a partner with you when you're out there, right?"

"If you want to call Eddie a partner, yes. At least he looks intimidating." She glanced toward the back of the house. "I have Hunter and I trust him completely. We've trained together for weeks now. I also trust my fellow team members. They're all good people."

"Okay, so we agree I have to keep out of your way and let you do what you need to do."

"Yes," she said. She put her hand in his, and

they shook. "I have to put it off for a couple of days anyway. I shot a man, and we have to clear that up first. Chief Jones says I need to see a counselor first thing tomorrow."

"A good idea," David replied. "Trust me on that. You'll have flashbacks and nightmares for a while to come."

Whitney didn't doubt that. She'd never forget that moment when she thought her baby might be killed. And she'd never forget David.

He tugged her into his arms. "Don't push me away, Whitney. I'm not like Brian."

Whitney should have pushed him away right then and there, but instead she hugged him close. "I know you're not. Lucas must have thought highly of you to send you here like this. So that means I care about you, too."

"I appreciate Lucas and his misguided mission," David said, "but this has gone beyond honoring Lucas. You might think you're too tough for someone like me but…we've both been through things that no one else can understand. For now, we need each other."

They held each other for a couple of minutes, and Whitney realized she hadn't been held or hugged like this in a long time. David was right. She did need someone she could trust.

"I miss my brother," she said. But right now

being in David's arms did not feel so brotherly. It felt right. Too right.

"Me, too," David replied. He held her with no demands, and he didn't try to make any advances. Could he see her fear, and feel it in his heart, too? "I miss his goofy laugh and his bad jokes. I miss how he talked about you all the time. Almost as good as being here with you."

Whitney absorbed some of his quiet strength and thanked God for David's sweet concern. But she prayed for her own strength and willpower to hold her steady so she wouldn't give in to these erratic, disturbing feelings she felt each time she was around him.

Pulling away, she looked up and into his eyes and saw the same hopes and fears she felt centered there in his powerful gaze. For a brief moment, she wanted to throw caution to the wind and kiss him. But…she had to control that impulse.

"You should go," she finally said. "You're worried about Miss Rosa, too, right?"

"Yep. You're right. I can't protect all of you."

"I could get in trouble for letting you ride along with me," she pointed out, making one last attempt to dissuade him.

"You could get in trouble if I don't ride along with you," he reminded her. "I can't see how anyone could argue with that."

After David left, Whitney checked the entire house to make sure all the doors and windows were locked, and she also checked in with James. As she was passing through the laundry room near the kitchen, she spotted Shelby's white bootie lying in front of the door to the garage.

"There you are," she said, lifting the bootie up. She must have dropped it when she'd taken it out of the laundry.

She turned one last time to stare into the backyard before she went to bed, and saw James and Hawk making their rounds. Blinking, Whitney moved through the house, intent on sleeping with her gun nearby.

Then the house phone rang. No one ever called her on that line, and it was strange to get a call this late at night. Her pulse puttering, Whitney picked up the receiver. "Hello?"

"We're watching you. Cute baby. Cute little booties."

Then the line went dead.

A chill ran down Whitney's neck and shivered toward her spine. Had someone been inside her house even before tonight?

THIRTEEN

On the way home, David shifted the ancient gears of the yellow Chevy, thinking he stood out like a school bus moving along through traffic. Checking the rearview mirror, he wondered if he was being watched right now. He glanced toward the Desert Valley Clinic and saw lights on.

Whirling the old truck into the parking lot, he thought he'd check around, just in case. But after what had happened hours earlier at Whitney's house, he planned to be very careful.

The front door was locked tight, so he walked around back to one of the big windows and saw Dr. Pennington in an exam room with a teenage boy. The kid was dirty, his pants torn, and he was bleeding from his left leg.

David checked the back door. Locked. So he knocked loudly.

Dr. Pennington opened the door, a surprised frown on his face. "Evans, what are you doing here?"

"I saw a light burning. Thought I'd see if everything was okay."

"Just get in here now," the gruff doctor said, motioning to the last exam room near the door while his gaze scanned the parking lot. "I've got a problem."

David turned toward the examining room. He might not like the doctor, but David had an obligation to help him as needed.

The doctor waved a gloved hand toward the young man writhing on the table. "He needs stitching, and I need you to assist."

David noticed the kid's fearful glance, his face twisted with pain. "What happened?"

Dr. Pennington gave David a stern stare. "We don't ask questions around here. We just do what we can."

"Looks like a knife wound," David said, memories of his first day in Desert Valley still fresh. "Should we report it?"

"Already did," Dr. Pennington replied on a tart note. "But the kid won't say anything. Can't press charges if we don't know what happened. He's afraid to talk."

He shot the kid a hard stare. The teen looked frightened and then lowered his gaze.

David took mental notes while he helped the doctor clean and stitch the deep gash slashing across the kid's left upper leg. This boy needed to go to the ER at the hospital. "Did you get into a fight?"

The teen ignored him, his jaw tight, his dark eyes darting here and there. He looked as if he could be high on something. Or maybe the doctor had given him something.

"He probably can't speak much English," Dr. Pennington said under his breath. "We do what we can, when we can. Best to keep your nose clean. Ask too many questions around here and you might live to regret it."

David couldn't decide if the scared kid was Latino or Native American or a mixture of both. But he had a sneaking suspicion the kid could understand everything they were saying.

When they were finished, the teen sat up and grabbed his bloody, dirty shirt. That was when David noticed the tattoo on his scrawny back.

It looked exactly like the symbol he'd had trouble remembering from the train attack. Was it the same? Or could it just be a coincidence?

He glanced at the tattoo, and then he looked into the black eyes of the teenager. The kid shot a furtive glance toward the doctor, who had his back turned.

Then he stared into David's eyes, a hidden plea shouting through his scared expression. David had seen that kind of plea in the eyes of children caught in the throes of war. Too many times.

"Where do you live?" David asked, hoping to encourage the boy to talk. "I'll give you a ride home."

The teen shut down again, his gaze moving back to the floor.

When Dr. Pennington turned around, the kid had the stoic, angry expression of someone who didn't want to be messed with.

And David had the distinct impression that the good doctor knew exactly what had happened to this teenager. So why had he insisted David stay to help? Maybe to give him a warning? Or to show him what happened when people saw things they shouldn't see?

"Hey, I heard about last Friday night. I'm so glad you're all okay," Gina, a junior dog trainer, said into the phone. "What can I do to help?"

"I need to run some errands," Whitney said. "I was wondering if you'd mind watching Shelby and Hunter for a couple of hours."

"Sure," Gina replied. "I'm on light duty myself these days, so I'd love a break. Want me to come to your house?"

"I'd feel better if you kept her at the training center," Whitney replied. "Hunter can have some play time, and Shelby should nap most of the time. Think Sophie will mind?" Sophie, the new lead dog trainer, was Gina's boss now.

"No. I'll keep Shelby in the apartment upstairs, where it's quiet and relatively safe. Now tell me about the other night."

"It was scary," Whitney replied, the nightmare still fresh in her mind a few days later. "But it was over so quickly, I'm still trying to absorb what happened. Killing a man is something I'll never forget."

"I can't even imagine. You run your errands and don't worry about us. But first, tell me more about what happened."

Whitney gave Gina some of the details of that night. Although Gina wasn't a K9 rookie, she was an excellent trainer who'd worked with Veronica Earnshaw. She was also newly engaged to rookie Shane Weston, but they hadn't announced that publicly yet, so Whitney knew to keep it to herself. Gina had tried to help piece together some of the details of Veronica's life.

"I've got some things to do today, so I appreciate the help. The Carters are pretty traumatized by what happened, so I'm letting them off the hook today."

She planned to do some checking on the rookie deaths, at least. She'd put it off for a couple of days, but now it was Tuesday and she was getting restless. "I talked to a counselor

Saturday morning, so that helped. But we're so shorthanded, I should be back on the job soon."

"I get it," Gina replied. "Hey, Shane said you and the medic seem to have a thing going on."

Whitney forced a chuckle. "He saw us together the other night right after this happened. We were both still in shock." Then she decided to be honest. "David knew my brother, so he's a good friend. He's checked on me all weekend, and he came by Sunday night for a visit."

"Since you've told a few people why David's really here, everyone is talking about how he promised Lucas he'd come here and find you. It's kind of romantic."

"Everything is romantic to you," Whitney pointed out. "You're in love."

"Yes, I am."

Whitney avoided any further discussion about David. Thankfully, Gina wasn't one to pry.

"I'm glad David was with you," Gina said. "But I sure don't like this coming on the heels of Veronica's death. First Ellen's mother gets hit over the head. Now someone's trying to get to you and David. And we still don't know what happened to little Marco. We need to find that puppy. I can't wait until the end of all this."

"You went through your own scare," Whitney said, thinking of the horror of Gina's troubled brother coming to Desert Valley and trying to kill her. But Tim was getting some much-needed help now.

"I'm okay," Gina replied. "Just glad it's over. I'm concerned about you now, though."

Whitney refused to be a coward. "I intend to catch the drug traffickers."

"Be careful," Gina warned. "You have a big target on your back after that train incident. Not to mention everything else we're dealing with."

"I will," Whitney replied. "I'll meet you at the training center."

"Okay. Hey, if you and the medic are growing close, more power to you."

"Thanks, Gina."

Whitney ended the call, wishing she could ask Gina for advice. Gina and Shane were engaged, and that was exciting. While she was happy for them, she wasn't ready to give in to having a man in her life again so soon after losing Brian.

But you never really had him, she thought.

She couldn't get involved with anyone until all of these dark clouds hanging over her head went away, starting with proving that Brian's death had not been an accident.

She dropped Shelby and Hunter with Gina and Sophie, giving her baby a big kiss and hug and a promise to be back in two hours. Then she headed toward the Desert Rose to pick up

David. Today she planned to go back over the burned remains of Brian's house, hoping to find anything that might give her a clue to what had happened the night of the fire.

Even though it had been over a year, the charred husk of the house hadn't been cleared yet. It was in an area that didn't get much attention from the county. Brian had liked the isolation of his little house near the river. She wondered if his land had been claimed by any relatives.

She'd gone back over the short list of people who knew Brian, but she still had no answers on old girlfriends or angry friends who'd realized he was a player. Brian had been a loner and he never talked about his friends or family much, so it would be hard to pin down anyone on that account.

When she pulled up to the Rose, David was sitting in one of the rocking chairs on the porch. He hopped up and hurried to get in the vehicle. "Miss Rosa is watching out the window on the pretense of making sure the patrol car comes by every thirty minutes. She thinks we're going for a romantic drive through the desert." He shrugged. "I didn't have the heart to explain we can't do that since we'd probably never make it home."

Whitney ignored the horror of that. "Does everyone around here think you and I are—"

"Yes," he said. "Miss Rosa wants you to find a good papa for your beautiful little girl."

A heated blush colored Whitney's face. The day was warm and getting warmer, but this heat came from within. "Why can't people understand I'm okay with being a single mother?"

David shot her a solemn frown. "Don't worry. I set her straight. Told her we're friends since I knew your brother." He stared out the window. "That is the standard response these days."

Whitney could tell her outburst bothered him, but his excuses to Miss Rosa bothered her. She didn't want his landlord to get the wrong idea. "It's not you, David."

"Right, it's you. You're still in love with a man who wasn't willing to make a commitment to you. A man who's been dead for almost a year."

This day wasn't starting off the way she'd planned. "I'm not in love with him. It's just that one thing after another has happened, and I haven't really had time to…mourn him. Not just his death but…the truth that was right there in front of me."

"Yes, so I get that maybe this quest to bring about justice will help you to heal and get on with your life."

"I'm trying to do that," she retorted. "I was on my way to finding out which police station I'd be assigned to when Veronica's murder took precedence, and then you showed up. Cut me some slack."

He looked sheepish. "I'm sorry. I've been on 'go' since I got off that train. I think we both need to relax and chill a little, don't you?"

"Sure, if we forget we've got drug runners gunning for us." Then she pointed a finger at him. "When we get to the house, just remember, you can't do anything or touch anything. It could mess with the chain of evidence and get it all thrown right out of court."

David let out a groan. "Maybe I should have listened to you and stayed out of this."

"I can let you out here," Whitney said, slamming on the brakes at a traffic light.

"No." David sat up. "Hey, we're both still on edge. Let's start over."

"Good idea." She smiled over at him. "I enjoyed the chocolate you brought over Sunday night."

"I'm glad you liked it."

Thirty minutes later, Whitney pulled up to the burned-out shell that had once been Brian's house, relieved that they hadn't been followed. Staring over at the blackened remains of the small cottage, she remembered laughing with

Brian, kissing him, giving in to all the impulses he brought out in her.

"Hey."

She didn't even realize she was gripping the steering wheel with a white-knuckled intensity until David's hand on her arm brought her back to the here and now.

"What?"

"Are you sure about this?"

"Yes," she said. "And I'm glad you're with me."

He looked relieved. "I wasn't sure you wanted me here."

Whitney took the keys out of the ignition. "I don't talk about Brian with anyone. It's too hard to explain, and I would hate the looks of pity I'd be sure to get." She eyed him. "Kind of like the way you're looking at me now."

David came around to meet her near the back of the SUV. "Hey, I don't pity you. I understand. I mean, I've seen all kinds of death, and in battle you learn to harden your heart against all the pain and suffering. You hide your emotions for so long, you forget how to feel. I think you're trying to do that. So I don't pity you. I admire you, Whitney. You're strong and brave and... you love your little baby. You faced down the world, accepted your lot in life and decided to overcome a bad situation and turn it into something good."

"Are you trying to make me cry?" she asked, touched that he could read her so easily. Touched that he saw how hard she'd fought to find her way alone.

"No." He pushed a hand over his clipped hair. "I'm trying to give you a compliment, but you're so shut down, you can't even accept that, either."

He was right. She didn't accept praise very well because she'd never thought she deserved praise. "Thank you," she said on a husky whisper. Then to add some levity, she asked, "Are we going to argue all day?"

"No." He nodded toward the skeleton of what was once a house. "Let's get this over with."

Whitney wanted nothing more than that. She hadn't been back here since the night they'd heard the report. She and her fellow rookies had watched as the fire department had gone over the house, searching for the source of the fire. When the fire inspector had found a burned-out cracked glass candleholder with the name of a prominent brand scorched but still readable on the glass, the department had deemed it as the source, since it had been located near what remained of the front window curtains.

Now the debris had been cleared and piled in the front yard. The house had been stripped down to the bare bones. It was an eyesore. And months had gone by. Almost a year. What was she doing here?

"I'm not sure what I'm looking for," she told David, her tone quiet. "It's a long shot, but I just needed to start here to get my bearings."

The house was located on a secluded, rutted road away from the surrounding neighborhood. Brian hadn't been much on yard work or decor, and the cute little stucco house had been simple and neat, with just enough room and privacy for a bachelor.

And the many women he'd brought here.

"It shouldn't take long to do a walk-through," she said, her shades pulled down to avoid the glaring midmorning sun. And maybe to hide her eyes. "I'm sure vandals have taken anything of value that was left."

She studied the blackened beams and singed carpet, went over what was left of the furniture and appliances. The fire had started up front, which was odd in itself. "If Brian had bought a candle, he wouldn't have put it near the door. Maybe on the coffee table or even in the bedroom. Why by the curtains?"

"What else was near the curtains?" David asked, scanning the worst of the burned areas of the house.

"Nothing," she said, memories charring her

brain in the same way the fire had scorched this house. "He had a table near the door where he placed the mail and some of his gear. It was near the hall closet, where he kept the lockbox for his gun. But that's over there." She pointed to the other side of the hallway, where the front door had been burned to a crisp. "That's away from the curtains. The remains of the candle were found near the window."

"Maybe the fire blew it off the table, or he threw the candle over there when he found the house on fire."

"I don't think he had time to do that. He was supposedly getting dressed for the police dance." She took a deep breath. "They found him just inside the bedroom door. He died of smoke inhalation." She closed her eyes, hoping he had passed out before the heat became too intense.

"Was his K9 partner here with him?"

"No." Whitney closed her eyes. "He'd left him kenneled at the training center. He did that sometimes when he knew he'd be out late." She touched the scorched remains of the couch. "His partner went to a police department in Winslow."

David moved through the tiny living area to stare into the bedroom. "Did you come here with him?"

"Yes," she said, glad she hadn't kept this a secret from David. Maybe because he hadn't questioned or judged her, she felt she could share things with him. "I came here a lot. Stayed here a lot." Then she stared over at David. "Obviously."

"And no one knew? I mean, could someone who was jealous have done this deliberately?"

"Possibly. He went through a lot of women. I'd heard rumors that he and Veronica flirted with each other while she was still married to Dr. Pennington."

"Wow." David stopped, his hands on his hips. "It's still weird that I found him at the clinic the other night stitching up that stab wound. And that the kid had the same sort of tattoo we've been seeing everywhere lately."

David had called her Saturday morning to tell her about that strange encounter. But the police department didn't have a report of an officer being alerted about the injured teen.

"Doc's known for helping those who can't pay and for going above the law to keep from having to deal with the police and the immigration officials. The teen could have been here illegally or…a drug mule."

"He seemed out of it, kind of high. I almost felt as though he wanted to say something to me, but he looked scared. I mean, really scared."

"Probably afraid he'd go to jail or be shipped back across the border," Whitney said. "Sometimes things are different here. Like when you were in battle and had to make snap decisions. Dr. Pennington does that a lot, too, I think."

She moved around, memories distracting her.

"The tattoo could match all the other symbols we've been seeing," David said.

"The doctor should have done a better job of reporting this. The department lets him get away with a lot."

"Okay, I'm reporting it to you," David said. "Just for the record."

"I've got it," she said, her eyes scanning the area by the door. When she saw something glistening near a pile of burned rubbish out in the yard, Whitney hurried over. With gloved hands, she pulled back the debris.

"I found something," she said, her heart lurching with both dread and hope.

Before she could say anything else, David threw his body over hers and held her down.

FOURTEEN

"David?"

"Sniper," he said, his breath coming in huffs. "I saw a flash up in the hills, just past the house."

Whitney lay still, believing him. "Can you see anything else?"

He lifted his head and scanned the hills off to the right of the house. "Hard to say." He moved his body a fraction. The whiz of a bullet hit about a foot from where they lay.

"I guess that answers that," he said, squinting toward the distant hills. "We're pretty much trapped."

"I can't breathe," Whitney said, the security of him protecting her bringing out more emotions and awareness than she cared to admit. "Let me up."

He moved away, his gaze focused on the hills. "We can make a run for your SUV."

Whitney weighed that choice with calling for

backup. "Okay, I'll cover you. Can you get in and drive close so I can make it to the vehicle?"

"Yes."

She rolled and centered herself behind the pile of rubble, sweat now pooling between her shoulder blades.

David took the keys. "Ready?"

She nodded. "It's not locked. Just get in as fast as you can."

They counted to three, and he took off while she fired a round toward the hills. When return fire pinged all around her, she twisted to check on David. She heard the roar of the truck's motor and breathed a sigh of relief.

Through another round of fire, David brought the truck to a skidding stop close to the burned-out shell of the house and opened the SUV door. Whitney fired another round and crawled toward the waiting vehicle.

Soon she was inside, and David was spinning out of the deserted yard. The shooting had ended.

"Did you get the bracelet?" he asked after he made sure she was okay.

Whitney held up the tarnished piece of jewelry and let out a breath. "Yes. Held on to it while I fired shots."

David's expression showed relief and appreciation. "Is it yours?"

"No. I've never seen it before. But I can tell you this—Brian didn't allow me to leave any jewelry or clothing here. He didn't like clutter, especially feminine clutter."

"Maybe someone dropped it on her way out," David replied, his eyes on the silver charm bracelet. "And...if she lost it out here, the investigators obviously missed seeing it."

"It seems that way," Whitney replied. Holding the tarnished, dirty bracelet up in the light, she added, "Whoever wore this could also be the same person who set this fire. Possibly the person who just shot at us, too."

"So you've accomplished something," David replied. "And we didn't die doing it, thankfully. What now?"

"I bag it and tag it," she said, careful that she didn't break the delicate thread that might hold the truth. "And...we report that we were shot at once again."

"It's escalating," he said, taking her hand in his. "We need to stick closer together."

Whitney saw the reasoning in that comment, but she couldn't be around David 24/7. Too tempting.

"The chief has just about run out of people to cover us," she said. "We might have to be on our own for a while."

She should have felt some sense of relief and

accomplishment after finding the bracelet, but being shot at so soon after killing that man in her house had ruined that buzz. Instead, she felt sick to her stomach and full of even more questions and doubts.

Who had dropped this bracelet?

And would she ever be able to find that person, or would she have to leave this as evidence and never find her answers?

Tuesday morning, Whitney reported to work again, went to Chief Jones and showed him the bracelet she'd found. "This is it, Chief. This bracelet seemed out of place at that house."

The chief's heavy eyebrows winged up. "Seriously, Godwin? That's all you've got? Some lookie looker combing over the ashes could have lost that piece of jewelry there."

"I'm sending it to the state lab for testing," she said. She couldn't tell him that since she knew Brian from experience, her gut was burning with the knowledge that someone had accidentally left the bracelet. "I wish I could find the woman who lost this."

"It's a long shot," the chief said. "But I guess we have to cover every angle. Send it on and keep me informed."

"Yes, sir." She'd already reported what the neighbor had told her about Melanie's habit of walking the same trail home on a regular basis, and now she added that she planned to go back over Mike Riverton's files, too. "And I'll go back over the fire report on Miller's house. Maybe we'll hit on something."

"You're dedicated, I'll give you that," Chief Jones said. "You'll make a top-notch investigator." Then he took off his glasses and gave her a fatherly stare. "If you don't get shot."

"It's hard to guess when they'll strike next," she admitted. "But I appreciate the patrols you've set up at the inn and around my neighborhood."

She left the chief's office and placed the envelope on her desk until she could get it to the lab. Then she went on with her day. After going over reports and checking for any new details regarding Veronica's death, she glanced up and realized it was lunchtime.

She met Ellen Foxcroft, the other female rookie, on the way to the break room. "Hey, how's your mother?"

"Still in a coma," Ellen said, her fatigue evident in her blue eyes. "We've still got guards at her door. I'm worried that whoever did this will return and try something else."

They walked into the break room and found Carrie Dunleavy, the police department secretary, sitting at a table, munching on some chips.

She looked up through her horn-rimmed glasses. "Hello, ladies. I brought brownies. Well, actually, they're blondies but...still good."

"Hmm, sounds yummy," Ellen said. "How ya doing, Carrie?"

"Can't complain," Carrie replied, her shy smile making her look cute. "How's your mom, Ellen?"

Ellen repeated what she'd told Whitney while Whitney heated up some soup and found her sandwich in the refrigerator. Ellen grabbed a banana and her yogurt and sat down across from Carrie.

"How are you?" Ellen asked Whitney, a concerned expression on her face.

"Okay," Whitney replied, not mentioning being shot at or finding the bracelet. "I'm doing all right, but I did go over some of these reports on Veronica's death. I thought maybe I'd hit on a clue or find a good tip."

"And what about this new man in your life?" Ellen asked with a soft smile.

Carrie looked up with interest and then shoved the plastic container of caramel-colored brownies toward Whitney. "Tell us. We want details."

"I guess word gets out around here," Whitney replied. Grabbing one of the moist dessert bars, she said, "You've all heard David knew my brother and served with him in Afghanistan. He's a medic. He was with Lucas when he died, so he came here to meet me."

Carrie sat up, her eyes going wide. "Wow, so it is true. That's so romantic. I mean, I know you lost your brother, and I'm so sorry, but for his friend to come here to see you—that's so sweet. He must have been close to Lucas."

Ellen gave Whitney an apologetic glance while Carrie blushed a bright pink. "I didn't mean to stir all of that up."

"It's okay." Whitney replied. "He and Lucas were close. Lucas convinced him to come and see me. But David and I are just friends. Nothing more." She shrugged. "He won't be here for long anyway."

Carrie's embarrassment changed to curiosity. "Is that the guy who came to look at mug shots that night? He's a hunk."

Whitney and Ellen both laughed. "Yes, he is," Whitney said, unable to deny it. "He's a nice man and a good medic. He'd make a great doctor one day."

They moved on to other topics. When Whitney finished and cleaned up her lunch, Carrie came to the sink and touched her on the arm.

"I'm glad you have a new friend, Whitney. Maybe one day I'll find a friend like that."

Then Carrie turned and hurried out of the break room.

Whitney again told herself that the next time she had one of her girls' night get-togethers, she'd invite Carrie, too. The secretary worked hard for all of them, and she really cared about the whole team. But it didn't look as though they'd have any downtime for a while.

It was a shame that they were all so closed off and private, but being a police officer did that to a person. She thought of David and how her feelings for him were changing from friendship to…something more. Something she wasn't sure she was ready for. Would she ever be able to hand her heart over to anyone again?

"Is this the symbol?" Whitney asked David on Wednesday morning.

David looked at the photo and nodded. "It looks like it, yes."

Hard to believe he'd been in Desert Valley for almost two weeks now. He'd grown closer to Whitney and he'd settled into a routine at the clinic, but he was tired of being stalked by bad people. He couldn't leave until he knew with certainty that those drug couriers wouldn't hurt Whitney or little Shelby.

"David?" Whitney waited for him to say something else. When he didn't, she prompted him. "Does it look like the one you saw on the teen in the clinic?"

"Close. Yeah, I'd say they were almost the same."

"It matches the one I spotted on the courier's arm," Whitney said, making notes.

"And I saw it on the SUV," David replied. "I'd say we've established it as some sort of emblem or totem."

He glanced up at Louise Donaldson. Louise was an older patrol officer who now seemed to be mostly on desk duty, according to Whitney, so she'd been doing research to help. She'd already confirmed that neither the 911 dispatcher nor the department had received a call from Dr. Pennington regarding a knife wound. He'd lied to David about reporting the kid's injury.

"Here's what I've found online," Louise said. "Dealing with criminals around here, I come across a lot of emblems and amulets. I've found some tattoos like the one you're describing, so let me pull them up for you to compare."

"Louise is good at this," Whitney had told him when she'd called him last night. "She can unearth all kinds of things. She's found her niche in doing background checks and research on cases for us."

Tall and solid, Louise wore her brown hair in a no-nonsense short bob that only made her brown eyes look even bigger. "So…you think this is it?"

"I can't be one hundred percent sure," David admitted while he studied the symbol, "but it's close." He'd looked at a lot of feather symbols, but this one stood out. "I guess the tattoos could vary, but the arrow with the three feathers was definitely on the kid's arm. And it looks like what I glimpsed on the SUV, too."

"The kids love to get symbolic tattoos," Louise said. "Thinks it makes 'em look cool. It could mean they've been inducted into some sort of drug smuggling operation, too. Young mules and couriers who'll likely die young. Probably why the kid was so scared. And the doc, too. If either of them squealed, they could both be buried in the desert."

David thought about how Dr. Pennington had acted. "The boy was scared. The doctor just seemed aggravated. But he did lie about reporting it, so maybe he was afraid he'd get caught in the middle of things."

"He works too hard," Louise replied while she scanned some other templates of local tattoos. "That can make a person ornery." She chuckled and nodded. "I'm counting the days myself."

Whitney and David studied the arrowhead symbol again. "It has three feathers," Whitney said. "That could mean something. Three branches or territories maybe?"

Louise bobbed her head. "Good guess. In Native American folklore, the feather represents honor and bravery, strength and power, and it's only given or worn to reflect those things. In this case, someone could be using it in an unscrupulous way that has no honor, but it could wield a lot of intimidation and power. In Spanish, it could mean *tres plumas*. Simply *three feathers*. That term has been around for centuries in one form or another."

"I've seen enough," Whitney said. "David?"

"This could be it," he said, still unsure. "It's close." Then he looked up at Whitney. "Will it help, or is this just a common thing around here? We didn't find a tattoo on the man you shot the other night."

"And we haven't identified him yet," Louise reminded them.

Whitney studied the screen, her long blond hair falling against her shoulders. She rarely wore it down, but today she'd left it pulled back just enough for some of the silky strands to cluster around her face, and it was distracting him big-time.

"It's a beginning," she said. "Since we haven't been able to identify the two men from the train or the one I shot, we can try to connect this symbol to them. And meantime, I'll call the state lab to push them along on the evidence we sent to them—the torn pants material and the weapon. Maybe they've heard something on our John Doe, too."

David thought of something else. "I could check the clinic records to see if Dr. Pennington's treated anyone else—say, someone who suffered a dog bite or stabbing—in the time I've been around."

"If he treated one of our guys, he probably wouldn't have left any trace of a report or record behind," Whitney said. "He seems to do things his own way."

"Or…he's being threatened," Louise pointed out.

David wasn't buying it, but Whitney looked thoughtful. "Don't go Rambo on me, okay?"

"I'm not planning on getting into trouble," David replied. "But I can check records and look around."

Louise's inquisitive gaze moved between David and Whitney. "What about train schedules? Have you confiscated the passenger log from that day?"

"Yes," Whitney said. "But the names don't match the description of these two, and no one along the route remembers them. We can't find them on any video surveillance, either. I figure they use fake IDs and heavy disguises and change things up at each stop they make. It's frustrating."

Louise read over the reports. "Let me see if I can establish a pattern. You know, match reports on drug smuggler arrests from other towns to what we know about ours. They might change things all the time, but sooner or later, they'll mess up."

"You are amazing," Whitney said to Louise. "I owe you a good cup of coffee."

"And a piece of cheesecake," Louise replied with a smile.

"You've got it. I'm ordering lunch, so I'll get it now." Whitney glanced at David. "Want to hang around? I'm eating lunch in to be safe."

"Sure," David said. "I don't have to be at the clinic until the late shift. Doc requested I work during some of the after-hours shifts."

She glanced over a menu from the Cactus Café. "They deliver, and this time we'll make sure it's the right person." After she'd placed their orders, she turned to David. "Hey, you ever thought about staying here and *working* at the clinic?"

David's gut burned with anxiety and awareness. He'd stay in a heartbeat if he knew she'd be staying here, too. But she'd made it clear she wanted to go back to Tucson.

"I'd have to think about it," he replied. "But hey, I'm wide-open for suggestions."

Surprise made her cornflower-blue eyes widen. "I guess you do have a lot of options."

David wondered if she thought of herself as one of those options.

FIFTEEN

Whitney accepted that part of her job involved waiting. It took time to get evidence back and to get lab reports, too, since they had to send everything to Flagstaff. But she was growing impatient. She had hoped to be in Tucson by now, living in a new place and getting adjusted to a bigger police department.

Instead, here she sat with a man who'd appeared in her life at the worst possible time.

Or…had David come at the best time?

The minister had talked about timing in church Sunday. He'd mentioned waiting on God's time. But that was hard to do, Whitney decided now, Hunter at her feet. Her impulsive, impatient nature had caused her to move too quickly with Brian. And she'd made mistakes in her first days as a rookie because of both of those things, too.

She had to be careful with David.

But when he smiled at her and settled his

loose-limbed body into the chair across from her desk, she had to wonder if God hadn't timed this one just right.

She was beginning to care about David. A lot.

Would God send him here only to take him away?

Or should she jump at this opportunity to find true happiness?

"What are you thinking?" David asked, his eyes scanning her face.

She couldn't tell him that. "Shrimp tacos," she said instead. "Can't wait to eat lunch."

He smiled. "I don't believe that, but we'll go with it."

After their lunch had been delivered, he leaned in and asked, "Do you feel as if we're still being watched?"

"Yes. I can't relax even stuck inside the police station. It's creepy, but what can we do?"

"Keep plugging away," he said. "Hope we find the people running drugs through Desert Valley."

"And the person who might have murdered four people," she said. Then she twisted her napkin. "This isn't a very fun lunch, is it?"

"Well, we tried a real date, and you know how that ended."

"Yes, I do." The thought of something happening to Shelby terrified her. The Carters were being diligent by keeping their children close and watching over Shelby, a patrol car parked on the curb.

David tapped his fingers on the old desk. "Hey, we need to talk about us."

"What about us?" she asked, glancing around, her heart doing odd little bumps and beats.

"Whitney, I…like you. A lot. I wonder what it would be like not to have to look over our shoulders for criminals chasing us, to be friends, to get to know each other more. To be together without any threats hanging over our heads."

Her shivers of apprehension turned to shivers of delight. That would be amazing, so nice. Wonderful. "I don't know," she admitted. "I've made so many mistakes."

"Hey, this isn't a mistake," he said, his brown eyes turning as rich and dark as the mocha brownies Carrie had brought in this morning. "My feelings for you can't be wrong. And I think you feel something for me, don't you?"

Whitney swallowed, her throat dry. "I—"

"How's it going?"

Whitney glanced up to find Ellen grinning at them.

"Good," she said, her gaze clashing with David's. "Kind of lying low."

"Okay," Ellen said. She nodded at David, grabbed an apple and kept going.

Whitney looked into David's eyes. "I have to eat and get back to work," she said on a hurried whisper. "Hunter needs a bath, so I'm taking him by the training center this afternoon. They have a huge shower that all the dogs love."

"Okay, then," David said, disappointment shifting through his gaze. Grabbing a taco, he bit in and chewed. Then he put it down and wiped at his fingers. "Dinner Friday night, at the inn. Bring Shelby and Hunter if you want, so you won't worry about anything. We should be safe with a patrol car on the watch."

"All right," she said, barely able to eat. "Another real date?" Then she shrugged. "I mean, if it is, maybe it should just be the two of us."

David's expression heated up at that comment. "Ah, something tells me the rookie is beginning to like me."

"I do like you and...I'd like a real date with you," she admitted, relieved to be honest with him.

"This will be as real as it gets," David said. "And ideally, no one will try to shoot us."

"C'mon, boy. Time for your bath."

The welcoming sound of yelping puppies echoed around Whitney and Hunter as they headed for the vet office.

Whitney moved through the big training yard

and entered the building near the puppy yard, her mind on poor little Marco. The missing puppy might be just fine, but she couldn't help but worry. It was well over a month and a half since Veronica's murder and still no sign of the puppy. She hoped someone who loved animals had found the little shepherd. Since Veronica put ID chips in all the puppies she trained, it was possible that Marco had one a vet could easily read. But no one had reported finding him.

Hunter spotted the door she was about to enter and glanced up at her with a hopeful expression. He seemed to enjoy getting a bath now and then, and he really didn't mind visiting the vet too much since Tanya Fowler, the center's veterinarian, always gave Whitney treats for him. Whitney liked to bathe him here in the big industrial tub and shower located in the hallway of the vet's office. Easier than trying to get him clean in the tub at home. Since he got into all kinds of things while on duty, it also saved her having to scrub down her bathroom.

"Hey, Whitney," Tanya said, her eyes lighting up at the sight of Hunter. "Hi there, Hunter. How ya doing?"

Hunter sniffed Tanya's knuckles but stayed by Whitney.

"Hi. He needs a bath," Whitney said. "Is it too late for me to give him one today?"

Tanya fluffed Hunter's coat. "Nah. Just lock up after you're done. You know the drill. Sophie's out in the yard, so she'll be around."

Sophie Williams had worked under Veronica's iron fist, and after Veronica's death, she'd immediately been promoted to lead trainer. She was doing a good job. But the pressure of the job and the implication that she'd killed Veronica had made her a little distant lately. Whitney didn't believe for a minute Sophie had murdered Veronica, even though the two colleagues had had their moments.

Veronica had not made life easy for anyone around her, and Sophie and she had gone a few rounds, but Sophie was dedicated to her work. From what Whitney had heard and seen, Sophie had been genuinely upset when they'd found Veronica. Whitney couldn't see her being involved in such a heinous act.

"I'll let her know I'm here," Whitney said.

"I'm on my way out there, so I'll tell her you're inside," Tanya said.

"Thanks, Tanya."

"You're welcome," Tanya said, her strawberry blonde curls swishing around her face. "Still no word on little Marco, huh?"

"Nope." Whitney guided Hunter toward the open shower and turned on the gentle spray to adjust the water temperature. "I've canvassed just about every neighborhood near where he was last seen. Someone took him. I wish we knew who and for what purpose. To keep him? To sell him?" Or worse—as some sort of memento because maybe it was Veronica's killer who had taken him, Veronica's killer who witnesses had seen on the bike?

"I hope he turns up," Tanya said. "Good to see you. I'll keep my eyes open for little Marco."

"Thanks," Whitney said. "C'mon, Hunter. We need to hurry up and get home to Shelby."

Hunter's ears perked up at Shelby's name. He loved the baby almost as much as he loved working. Soon Whitney had him lathered up and enjoying a good, clean blast of warm water on his short, lush fur. "Nice, huh?"

After giving Hunter a good rinse, she heard a door opening and figured Sophie was calling it a day. "Wanna say hi to Sophie?"

He glanced around and then growled low.

"Hunter? What's wrong, boy?"

Whitney felt it, too. The hair on the back of her neck stood up. Afraid to look around, she hurried to finish up with Hunter. "It's okay, boy," she said to calm the dog. "Stay."

Hunter kept looking beyond the hallway, out toward the puppy-training-yard door.

"Sophie, is that you?"

No response.

Grabbing a huge towel, Whitney turned off the spray and quickly toweled Hunter. The big dog shook off the moisture but became more agitated with each second that ticked by.

"Stay," Whitney commanded on a gentle note. She thought she heard a sound. Footsteps? A door creaking open down the hallway?

"Who's there?"

No one answered, but Hunter kept growling. Whitney commanded Hunter to calm down, but she drew her gun all the same. Leashing the still-damp K9, she whispered, "Search."

Hunter did his job, moving toward the door to the puppy yard. They passed storage closets and kennels, but Hunter stopped at a closed door near the open yard outside. Whitney held her weapon in front of her, her other hand on the knob. But before she could turn the knob, the door opened with a swish of force that sent her flying backward. She hit her head on a metal cabinet, the pain jolting through her while Hunter's barks echoed throughout the building.

Suddenly, the door from the inside training area opened, and Sophie hurried up the hallway. "Whitney?"

Whitney blinked, dizziness overcoming her. She saw a dark shadow dressed in black pushing out the door to the yard, Hunter snarling and dancing around her as the door slammed shut. Then she passed out.

"Whitney?"

She opened her eyes to find Sophie leaning over her.

Touching her head, she asked, "What happened?" Then she realized she was no longer at the training center.

"Someone knocked you down," Sophie said. "Stay still. You're at the clinic in an examining room."

"Hunter?"

"He's safe. He wanted to go after them, but I held him back. The whole team is searching the yard and buildings."

Whitney tried to sit up. "Shelby?"

"We've sent Ryder to check on her. It's okay. Just stay still."

Whitney tried to sit up again, but another door burst open and she heard voices, then a man issuing an order.

"Let me check on her."

David. Of course he was here. He'd been on his way to the clinic earlier.

He came into focus, concern marking his steely expression. "Hey, how you doing?"

"Head hurts."

She shouldn't be so glad to see him, but she was. Or maybe she was still dreaming.

"You might have a concussion," he said, his fingers moving gingerly over the back of her head. "We'll get you checked out."

"I'm okay. Home. Shelby."

"Soon," he said, his tone gentle, his eyes full of concern.

Whitney nodded and closed her cycs while everyone around her went about their work. David probed and checked and examined and asked her questions, his hand gentle on her head.

"I want to go home," she told him. "I can't stay here, and I'm not going to the hospital. Shelby needs me." She grabbed his shirtsleeve. "David?"

An hour later, David had her lying on the couch at her house. "I'll be right here monitoring you," he said. "You need to stay up for a few hours."

"David," she said, taking his hand. "I can't get myself killed. Shelby needs me."

"I know," he said. "Shelby is safe. I'm here. But we need to step things up. The person who knocked you against that shelf got away. No place is safe around here."

Then he leaned down and whispered in her

ear. "Which is why I'll be here with you all night long."

Whitney didn't argue. This had escalated beyond the breaking point. They'd been threatened in both their homes, shot at over and over and now someone had breached the training center.

Drug traffickers or someone trying to sabotage the investigation involving Veronica's death? Either way, Whitney realized this might not be over for a while.

David waited until the clinic was quiet.

After making sure Whitney's concussion was mild enough that he could leave her with her neighbor Marilyn Carter, he'd agreed to work the late shift at the clinic today. Now he understood why Dr. Pennington had asked him to do so. The doctor had left early again tonight. David had bent the rules a lot in the middle of the battlefield. Having to make snap decisions meant the difference between life and death. But here, it was a whole other kind of triage.

The place was a mess. Nurses coming and going, quitting and coming back, a doctor who was brilliant at his job but not so diligent with protocol or his bedside manner, and too many sick, hurting patients who didn't have insurance or the money to pay. He almost wished he could just take over and get things in order.

But…that couldn't happen, could it? He didn't think Dr. Pennington was going anywhere soon. David wasn't sure he had enough fight in him right now to do more than try to help the patients.

David had a small window of opportunity to do a little snooping, and then he'd get back to Whitney. He carefully checked the medicine cabinets and made sure no drugs were missing. Everything looked in order there. He'd ventured into Dr. Pennington's office a couple of times, but the doctor kept things tidy so nothing could look out of place. Besides, he wasn't even sure what he was looking for.

David moved silently down the empty hallway, careful to watch the parking lot as he entered Pennington's office. The big mahogany desk centered inside had several folders stacked on one side, an ink pad and calendar in the middle and some textbooks on the other side. On one wall, a set of bookshelves housed more textbooks and medical tomes along with hunting pictures and a few scattered artifacts. Apparently Dr. Pennington loved the great outdoors.

David moved past the bookcase and tried opening the top-right drawer of the desk, but it was locked.

That figured.

Then he pulled open the bottom drawer and

was surprised to find a handgun hidden underneath some prescription pads and other papers. Well, that didn't make the doctor a criminal. This clinic could be a dangerous place if a drug addict showed up, demanding supplies. Having a weapon on site was probably a good idea.

Still…it was unusual to find in a doctor's office. David didn't touch the handgun, but he did note the details. A semiautomatic with an ivory handle. Nice weapon.

He picked up one of the folders and read over it. Nothing there. They'd treated an older man for dementia and suggested he find a specialist. Dr. Pennington had even called a colleague to give the referral. It was all right there. The other reports were in order, too. At least the man kept accurate records when it came to the everyday patients. But David was more concerned with the doctor's nefarious activities.

Frustrated, David couldn't pinpoint anything out of the ordinary. Maybe Dr. Pennington was just harried, but David's gut told him there was more to the doctor's mysterious ways than just being busy and under stress.

Maybe the doctor had a drug habit. The way he came and went with various people, his temper and mood swings, even his erratic behavior could point to that.

David got up to recheck the drug cabinet but

then he realized that if the doctor had a serious problem, he wouldn't take from the cabinet. He'd leave the clinic to meet his supplier. That had to be it. He could be buying drugs for personal use.

Deciding he'd have to start watching for more signs, David went back to the office. He looked up to find a vehicle pulling up behind the clinic, its headlights shining right into the office window. He grabbed a report and walked out just as the back door opened.

The doctor stood there glaring at him with an accusatory expression plastered on his face. "Evans, what are you still doing here?"

SIXTEEN

An hour later, David knocked on Whitney's door.

"Hi," Marilyn said, opening it with Shelby in her arms. "She's awake and waiting for you." Marilyn chuckled and tickled Shelby. "We all are."

After Marilyn had made it safely next door, he sank down in the chair beside Whitney sitting propped on the couch. Shelby played in her little fun kiddie bed nearby. "I'm sorry I had to leave for a while."

Whitney gave him a wry smile. "I think you had cabin fever after staying here last night and part of today."

"I did not. I've enjoyed being your…private doctor."

"I have to admit, I've enjoyed having you around. So has Shelby. Even Marilyn beams when you enter a room."

"I need to talk to you," he said, relieved to

see the color back in her face. Happy that she liked being with him.

Whitney settled against the couch and stared up at him. "Is everything okay?"

David saw Hunter positioned in front of Shelby's room in the hallway. The big dog gave him a curious glance and then laid his head on his paws. That was becoming an endearing sight.

And so was Whitney. She wore her hair down. It looked damp, so she must have just washed it. She had on a long DVPD black T-shirt and dark gray leggings.

"Everything's fine," he said. Then he moved to the couch and pulled her close, his fingers automatically moving over her head. "Just…a long day. I wanted to get back here. Right here."

Whitney hugged him but pulled away. "I'm fine. No more headaches and more energy today. But you don't look so hot. What's going on?"

"I think I might have something figured out," he said after checking her pupils.

Whitney pushed his hands away. "Stop examining me, David, and tell me what's going on."

He told her about almost being caught by Dr. Pennington. "I made up some excuse about looking over a patient file," he said. "I think he bought it, or maybe he pretended to believe me."

"What did you find?" Whitney asked.

"Nothing," he admitted, fatigue weighing heavy on his shoulders. "But I have a theory. I'm beginning to wonder if Dr. Pennington might have a drug habit."

Whitney gasped. "Have you seen him taking drugs?"

"No, nothing I can prove. The medicine cabinet is safe." He sat up and hung his hands together over his knees. "But he comes and goes at the oddest times. Sometimes he leaves in his sports car. Other times someone picks him up, and they leave for a while."

"Same vehicle as the one we saw?"

"I can't ever tell enough about it to compare it to the one we saw near the tracks, but I did manage to check it out a couple of times. No emblems."

"A dark SUV doesn't mean he's taking drugs."

"I realize that, since Dr. Pennington doesn't seem concerned about his friends pulling up to take him away. He trusts me way too much, too. I'm supposed to be a volunteer, but he's letting me handle a lot of responsibility that I really shouldn't be handling. If he's suspicious or scared, he sure doesn't act like it, and really, he keeps everything just within the law at the clinic."

"Maybe he's setting you up," Whitney suggested, a trace of fear in her words. "He could turn you in for something trivial just to make a point or get you out of his hair."

"Yeah, that did occur to me." He shook his head. "I'm gonna keep at it, though. His actions are too erratic to be normal."

"David, you don't have to do this. Maybe you should reconsider volunteering there."

"I have to find out what he's up to," he said. "Something's off, and with everything that's happened, I can't help but be involved."

Whitney propped herself up on her pillows again. "I wish you'd come to town under different circumstances."

"Yeah, me, too." David smiled at her. "I'm sorry."

She pushed at her hair. Her skin shimmered with a fresh-faced glimmer. "For what?"

"I rushed in here and unloaded on you without even asking you about your day."

"My day was boring," she said. "I rested as ordered, chatted with Marilyn since she sat with me all afternoon while her wonderful husband took care of her four children. Sleep a little, had a shower and talked to Gina about her hush-hush wedding plans."

She glanced toward the hallway and then moved her gaze to Shelby. "And enjoyed spending some quiet time with Shelby." Then she stared into his eyes. "I wanted to see you. Isn't that silly? I mean, I keep seeing that guy I shot, and I think about what could happen to Shelby or you. Then I think about the spot where I was attacked. That's almost the exact spot where Veronica died."

Seeing the distress in her eyes, David gave in and moved closer. Without hesitation, he wrapped her in his arms.

"Let's take a deep breath and talk about something else," he suggested while he enjoyed the sweet floral scent of her hair.

"Good idea," she mumbled. "Still nothing on the bracelet or the shooter, and I can't pinpoint anything from the fire report. I went back over Mike Riverton's file one more time, but I didn't find anything new. He was an expert mountain climber, and the official report has him falling down the stairs in his house."

"Let all of it go for a while," David said. "Have you eaten?"

"No, you?"

"No."

"Pizza?"

"Please." Then he lifted her chin with his index finger. "But we're still having our real date tomorrow night so don't try to get out of it."

"I won't. I can't wait."

"Miss Rosa is going all out."

She grinned up at him. "I'm glad you're here. I mean, I have friends from church, and the other rookies are my friends, but…it's different with you. I trust you, David."

"Is that because I knew Lucas, or in spite of it?"

"Both," she said, getting up before he could hold her close again. "Pepperoni or sausage?" she asked as she grabbed her cell phone.

"Both," he retorted with a wink.

But in spite of his high hopes, he had a feeling they wouldn't ever be able to relax completely until all the mysteries surrounding them were done and over.

"Godwin, I need you and Harmon in my office right now," Chief Jones shouted up the hallway on Friday. Whitney stopped and let out a sigh. All day, she'd tracked down tips and had phone conversations with everyone from kids messing with her and pranking the whole department to people telling her Marco had been taken by aliens who landed in the desert on a regular basis. She'd spent hours going over the reports on Brian's house fire and Mike Riverton's fatal fall down the stairs at his house again. And while she hadn't cracked anything, she had discovered that both Brian and Mike had something in common besides being rookies.

They'd both had blond hair, and they'd both been killed on the night of the police dance and fund-raiser.

These observations were known facts, but when she put them together and added that Melanie Hayes had also been killed that same night years before, things got weird all over again. But it was the blond hair of the two men that had her establishing a certain pattern.

Did the alleged killer have a thing for blond-haired cops?

Or did the killer hate all blonds? If so, why kill Melanie Hayes? Then she'd realized the obvious.

Ryder Hayes had blond hair, too.

Did they have a serial killer on their hands?

But one thing stood out more than anything else—this person had to have inside knowledge of the whole department. Even the frequency of Melanie's route home. Even the layout of Brian's house and the exact spot on Mike's stairs that could cause a fall.

She'd reported all of her findings earlier, but she hadn't discovered anything else that outstanding. She'd only reinforced that the killer had an established pattern.

"We might want to beef up security at the police dance this year, sir."

Chief Jones had agreed with that.

Now Whitney only wanted to go home and get ready for her big date with David. She'd even arranged for her friends Gina and Ellen to babysit Shelby and watch out for Hunter. Leaving her baby and her K9 partner with trusted colleagues made her feel better about going on this date. And it gave the Carters next door a break.

Turning, she gritted her teeth. "Yes, sir. What's up?"

"Louise has found something," the chief said as he stalked up the hall toward her. "Might be nothing, but she's been checking on passengers up and down the train line. We've put out an alert, and someone in Las Vegas saw a couple of suspicious-looking men boarding with large dark duffels. Two coach seats, no checked luggage and disembarking in good ol' Desert Valley in about an hour. Sent us an alert. We've established probable cause with our last find, and we're using a K9 for the search in a public place, so no warrant necessary. You know the drill. Don't harass the passengers, but do a sweep, get permission to search any private compartments if needed and see what you find in the storage areas."

Whitney glanced at the clock and then back to the chief. No way she'd be able to meet David on time, if at all.

"You got something important to do tonight, Godwin?" the chief asked, overly animated.

"No, sir. Nothing as important as this."

"Good. I'm sending you to search the train, and I'll have Weston and Harrison there with their K9 partners for backup."

"Why me, sir?"

"This is your case," the chief said. "You've been cleared to go back out there. Are you ready?"

"Yes, sir."

She hurried Hunter toward the patrol car, her cell phone in hand. Can't make it tonight. Work. The text to David would have to do for now. This could be the big break they'd all been waiting for on this drug case.

David read the text again.

Work. Tonight of all nights?

Well, he didn't have work tonight, because he'd made it clear at the clinic that he had plans.

Glancing around, he took in the bistro table Miss Rosa had set up on the long back porch for the two of them. A new security light made the whole yard glow, and the new gate had a solid lock on it. Plus a patrol car was parked in the alley.

"What do you think?" she asked now, her hands on her plump hips. "It's been a long time since we've had anything so romantic going on here, so I tried to make it special."

"It's very nice," David said, taking in the lush pink and yellow roses trailing down from a glass vase in the center of the table, the white cloth and silver utensils, crystal goblets and fine china. A latticework screen standing a few feet away kept the table secluded and private, while a ceiling fan whirled in a gentle motion overhead. "You've outdone yourself."

"Then, why so glum?" Miss Rosa asked. "The food is ready. Baked chicken with herbs, a salad, my famous cheesy potatoes and strawberries I hand dipped in chocolate. We're good to go."

"Not all of us," David said. "My date has to work late tonight."

Miss Rosa pursed her lips. "Oh, no. The nature of the job, honey." Patting him on the arm, she said, "I don't sleep well anyway. We'll wait for her and heat it all up, no matter how late."

Wait for her.

David wondered if he could do that. Wait for her, worry about her, try always to watch over her. He'd insult Whitney if he kept up with that. He couldn't protect her in the way Lucas had wanted him to. Whitney was too independent and stubborn for her own good, but those traits also made her a good police officer. Those traits attracted David to her but made it hard for him to give in to the attraction.

She wasn't the kind of woman who'd want to settle down to domestic bliss. And he wasn't even sure if he was that kind of man. He'd barely had time to think anything through over the past few months. He'd come here as a courtesy to a dying soldier, only to be thrust into the kind of adrenaline-filled world he'd left. He wasn't ready to rush headlong back into danger and death at every turn. He wasn't a coward, but he wasn't sure he wanted this kind of life forever.

Not with the woman he had so easily fallen for.

It might be time for him to leave Desert Valley.

He turned to Miss Rosa. "Thank you so much. I'll let you know if I hear from her."

But he wouldn't hear from her tonight, and he knew it. Whitney loved her work, and he appreciated that about her. But she was also obsessed with another man. A man whom she could mold and shape in her dreams to make him perfect, no matter how much he'd hurt her in real life. A dead man. Her child's father.

David couldn't measure up to that.

"I'm going for a drive," he told Miss Rosa.

The older woman reached out her arms. "I need a hug."

David hugged her tight, accepting that she saw he was the one who needed the hug. "Thank you, Miss Rosa, for everything."

Miss Rosa stood back and patted his arm. "You're a good man, David. She's a blessed woman to have you in her life."

David wasn't so sure about that, but he smiled down at Miss Rosa. "I'll see you later."

Then he hopped inside Miss Rosa's old pickup and headed north.

To buy a train ticket out of Desert Valley.

David turned onto the two-lane road leading to the train station, his mind whirling with what he had to do next. Traffic was light. As he rounded a curve, he spotted a familiar car up ahead.

The blue Camaro. The drug traffickers.

Disregarding everything he'd thought or decided since he'd seen Whitney's text, he started following the blue car. Keeping his eyes on the souped-up vehicle, David called 911 and reported seeing it. Whatever was happening, he planned to hang around and make sure Whitney was safe.

SEVENTEEN

Whitney pulled into the almost empty parking lot. She'd called Gina and Ellen to update them on the change of plans, that she was working instead of…going on a date. Whitney was grateful that Ellen, fellow rookie and a brave officer, would be at her home tonight, watching over both Gina and Shelby while Whitney was out.

"Be careful, Whitney," Ellen said. "We'll be fine here."

Eddie Harmon grunted beside her. "I had plans to go to a movie with my wife and grandchildren."

"I had plans, too," she shot back. She said goodbye and thanks to Ellen and pocketed her phone. "Let's check this out, and hopefully we can be done with these people."

Hunter stood on the seat, staring out the back window.

They exited the vehicle, and she leashed Hunter. "All right, let's get on with it." After she and Hunter had cleared the checked luggage compartment, she alerted the train conductor to leave all the exits shut except the one through which she and Hunter would enter.

"Harmon, you stand guard at that exit," she told Eddie. "No one on or off, understand?"

"Got it," Eddie replied with a grimace. They'd both put on bulletproof vests, just in case.

"Only a few passengers this trip," the conductor told Whitney. "I've alerted them to stay seated and to cooperate." He nodded for her to enter the open exit.

Whitney took a deep breath, the dust whirls moving through the sagebrush kicking up particles that tickled her nose. If this went the way she figured, she wouldn't have to dig through too much luggage. On the other hand, she really wanted to catch some drug couriers.

"Go," she commanded Hunter. "Search."

Hunter tugged at the leash and started doing his job. Lifting his head, he sniffed the hundreds of different scents in the stuffy train, moving by some people and stopping for a couple of seconds near others.

Whitney searched the faces of the half-dozen or so passengers. She didn't see anyone who looked like the two men she'd encountered the last time she'd been here, but then, she hadn't expected to see the same ones. They were either in hiding or dead. Their boss wouldn't be happy that they'd failed.

They moved on to the last two seats on the last row. According to the tip, the two suspicious men should have been in these seats. How had they gotten off the train without her seeing them? Hunter sniffed the seats on both sides of the aisle and then stopped, his whole body going rigid near the two seats in question.

"Find," Whitney urged, watching the exits.

Hunter pressed his front paws down and sniffed under the seat nearest the aisle. He barked and turned to stare at Whitney.

To make sure he wasn't giving her a false alert, Whitney encouraged him again. "Search."

Hunter crept down and pawed under the other seat, moving his snout over the floor area.

Whitney told him to stay, and then she let go of his leash so she could get down and check underneath the seats. She saw two black canvas duffels stuffed together. Dragging one out, she settled it across the seat. Hunter's excited frenzy increased, and he started pawing at the duffel.

Whitney opened it and found what she'd been looking for underneath a barrier of clothes and plastic garment bags. Party boxes. Not as many as before, but enough. She pulled out the other duffel, with the conductor and another staff member watching.

After taking out one of the packages, Whitney opened it with a box cutter and took a picture of the powdery white substance. Then she alerted Eddie Harmon so he could vouch for her find, called it in to the department, sent pictures and requested backup.

"Already there," the dispatcher reported.

"Do I have permission to remove this evidence from the train?" she asked the chief after she'd been patched through.

"Go ahead," Chief Jones said. "We'll alert the DEA to meet you at the site. Get those drugs off that train, but keep your eyes on them."

Whitney and Eddie carefully removed the duffels with gloved hands and tagged them as evidence. Then, after Eddie had pulled the car up alongside the tracks, they loaded them into the trunk of the Crown Victoria and took yet another picture. Both Shane Weston and James Harrison were doing a sweep of the other cars and the surrounding areas. They'd have to wait here for the DEA, but at least these drugs wouldn't make it to the streets.

But where were the couriers?

"I'll guard the stash and watch for the DEA," Eddie said. "The drug runners might still be hiding out somewhere in another car."

"Right." He made sense to Whitney, and he was actually doing his job. She commanded

Hunter to go, and they headed back onto the train. Now she started asking passengers about the two people who were supposed to be on the train along with the duffels, all the while checking each person for disguises or nervous twitches.

"I saw only one person sitting near that spot," an older lady replied. "He was tall, with dark hair, and he was wearing a cowboy hat and dark shades. But he got off at the stop before this one and never got back on."

After several passengers had verified that, Whitney figured someone had tipped the courier. But why hadn't he taken the duffels? Maybe someone else was supposed to board the train to retrieve them?

The passengers were beginning to grow restless, but she couldn't let this train leave until all the cars had been cleared. When Hunter alerted at one of the closed bathroom doors, Whitney motioned for the train employees to back away. The bathroom appeared to be occupied.

"Police officer," she called out. "Anyone in there?"

Hunter seemed to think so. Or he smelled the scent of someone who'd been here recently.

Whitney jiggled the door and it fell open. The bathroom was empty. Deciding one of the couriers had managed to get to the bathroom and hide before she got on the train, she figured he'd somehow managed to sneak out before all the doors were shut.

They didn't find anything or anybody, so she thanked the officials and exited through the one open door where she'd started.

Then she heard gunshots.

David heard shooting.

Whirling outside the train station gift shop, he looked for the man he'd followed into the ticket office. David was almost certain he recognized the man as the same one driving this car once before. Where had he gone?

The man had parked the blue Camaro. David noticed the tattoo on his left lower arm. The arrow pointed up, with the three feathers dangling below the arrowhead. The tattoo looked almost exactly like the one he'd seen on the SUVs and on the injured teen. He was pretty sure this man was disguised but...he looked a lot like the taller of the two who'd attacked Whitney the first time.

When the shots rang out, David spotted two K9 officers hurrying toward the front of the train.

And then he saw Whitney moving through one of the cars.

He had to warn Whitney. But the rapid fire of

more gunshots going off had everyone around him scurrying for cover.

Running out of the train station, he saw the Crown Victoria pulled up close to the track on the other side, facing the train, and Eddie Harmon crouched down beside the open trunk. Sweat pouring off his face and shock in his eyes, Harmon had his weapon trained on the sparse woods past the train station. And he was bleeding from the shoulder.

Harmon spotted David and waved him back. "Get out of here."

"Hang on," David called back. "I'm coming to check on you." Lifting up, he searched for Whitney. Another round of shots whizzed through the air.

"Get down," Harmon called, his face pale. But he was watching the woods. Holding his shoulder, he shook his head. "I'll be fine. Go find Whitney."

"Where is she?" David asked. Off in the distance, he heard sirens. An officer and a K9 ran toward the train station. He recognized Ryder Hayes and his K9 partner, Titus. Then another K9 officer and former soldier Tristan McKeller walked up with his yellow lab, Jesse. Tristan had a high-powered rifle with him.

"Don't know," Harmon called out in answer to David's question. "But…we got a sniper or two out in those hills past the train tracks. Got me good before I knew what was coming."

Almost the same spot where they'd taken Whitney last time. Would they get away with yet another shipment?

David prayed he was wrong and asked God to protect Whitney.

But he didn't plan on waiting, so he skirted the train cars. When he saw her running up the side of the train with her gun drawn and Hunter beside her, he eyed the woods and then eyed the distance between Whitney and Eddie Harmon.

If he could get to the other side of the tracks, he'd be able to watch the woods and maybe locate the sniper. And distract him enough to get Whitney to safety.

When another shot rang out, followed by Harmon's return fire, David crouched low and took off. He slid in beside Eddie Harmon as another shot whizzed by and hit a rock about ten feet away.

"Might be more than one," Harmon shouted into the radio. He didn't even bother fussing at David. "I can't see anyone. I'm in possession of the confiscated packages. Injured but still up."

In spite of his protests, David did a quick check of Eddie's shoulder. "A through and through," he told Eddie. "Are you okay for now?"

Eddie nodded, his face white and sweaty.

"I've had worse mowing the yard. Hurts like a scorpion sting, but I'm good for now."

David lifted up to look for Whitney. He heard Hunter barking and saw her crouched down the way, between two cars.

He couldn't get to her. David didn't mind the danger for himself, but he'd be a hindrance if he tried anything and distracted her too much.

A hindrance. This situation only reinforced his earlier decision to leave. He was a medical professional, and even though he'd been trained for combat, he did not want to stand in the way of the woman he cared about because she was an officer.

But when Whitney made it back to the open door of the train car, which still held several passengers, he watched as she ordered Hunter, "Guard." When she left Hunter in front of the open door and started running toward the woods, he realized she was going to backtrack to get to the shooter. Alone.

David gave Eddie Harmon a determined glance, turned and took off back across the track. He couldn't let her go out there alone, and Harmon was pinned down and injured. David did know a thing or two about rescuing people under fire, but he only hoped he wouldn't witness Whitney getting gunned down.

He hurried around the train and came up

on the perimeter of the area where the sniper seemed to be embedded. The arid area around the tracks consisted of sagebrush and cacti, ponderosa pines and deep gullies and dry, gutted washes.

Whitney was a sitting duck out there on her own.

Whitney pressed against the hot train, bullets whizzing past her head while the fumes from the idling engine engulfed her in an oily smelling fog.

She could hear return fire, thankful that Eddie was okay and apparently firing back.

But she had two train cars between the police vehicle and her, and she had to make sure Hunter didn't get caught in the cross fire. He'd guard the passengers unless she told him to move, and he'd make sure no one left that train car or got into it, but he was still exposed.

She lay against the dusty earth, watching the rocks and trees off in the distance, assessing that one man had gotten off the train earlier while the other one had hidden in the bathroom and slipped out undetected. Then she heard barking and voices calling out commands. Her team was organizing a perimeter. Now if they could figure out how to subdue the shooter without getting anyone killed.

* * *

David made it to the back of the train without getting hit. He'd been careful to belly crawl slow and steady against the dry shrub brush and the hard brown sandstone. His jeans scraped against rocks and cactus shrubs, and his elbows ached from scratches and slides, the burn of raw skin reminding him of being pinned down on a vast mountain on the other side of the world, injured men moaning and crying out all around him.

For a moment, he was back there, praying and trying desperately to save one of them.

David shut his eyes to the burning that pricked at him with a piercing agony worse than any cactus thorn. Here, with Whitney caught in a trap, he realized why he couldn't take that next step and give in to his feelings for her.

He didn't want to live through this kind of pain ever again. If he stayed, he might have to do this over and over, even if it was in his nightmares.

When he heard more gunfire, David forced his eyes open and saw that he wasn't in Afghanistan and there were no wounded, crying soldiers around him.

There was only the hot desert sun and one brave woman trying to protect everyone.

He wasn't going to let her do it alone, no matter how reckless and stupid his actions might seem. But he wasn't going to die, and neither was she.

God had brought him here. God would see him through.

He clung to that hope as he watched the distant woods and finally saw the glint of the sniper's gun. David slid along beside the tracks, finding rocks and shrubs to shelter him. Careful to look before he reached, he checked for rattlesnakes hiding in the rocks and crevices.

In what seemed like hours but had only been minutes, he made it into the outcropping covered in shrubs and bushes across from the last car of the train. Squinting into the sun, he saw several officers converging up the way, but the sniper—or snipers—were holding them in a standoff.

He was about to make his move toward where he thought the sniper was hiding when he saw Whitney doing the same thing he'd been doing—crawling her way toward the woods.

Not good.

David had to make a move before the sniper spotted her.

He reached a worn trail near some saplings and tumbleweeds and slid up behind a jutting rock formation.

And heard the click of a gun behind his head.

EIGHTEEN

"Godwin, talk to me. What's the status?"

Whitney had to answer Chief Jones. "I'm on the ground near the middle train car," she replied. "One, possibly two, shooters to the northwest through the woods. Hunter is guarding the occupied train car. Eight passengers inside, sir."

"Hang on, Godwin. We're gonna get you outta there."

"Yes, sir."

Whitney squinted into the woods. Sweat poured into her eyes and she blinked. Once. Twice. Then she saw it. Two men walking toward the train.

Her heart tripped over itself as she spoke into her radio. "Sir, we have a situation."

"You mean worse than the one we're already in?"

"Yes, sir." She lifted up and tried to get a good look. Pulling down her dark shades, she slid up against the locomotive and watched the dust kicking up behind the two crouched men.

David!

They had David out there.

"Godwin, report!"

"They have a hostage, sir." She swallowed and described David. "I think it's David Evans."

Chief Jones shouted down the line. "We have a hostage situation. Stand down."

Wondering how this could be possible, Whitney watched as the man holding David at gunpoint marched right up to the edge of the woods and stared over at her, using David as a shield.

Whitney crouched on one knee and held her gun out. "Let him go. Now!"

"I don't think that's gonna work," the man said through a dry cackle of laughter. "We tried to warn you."

The man had a dark beard and wore a cowboy hat. He must have been on the train at one point. The witnesses had described him. Whitney felt sick to her stomach. The drug dealers had tried to outsmart her. But they hadn't planned on Whitney getting a solid tip.

"Look, your beef is with me and the police department," Whitney said as the man drew closer. "Let him go."

"Can't," the man replied, the gun digging into David's ribs. "I have my orders."

"And what orders are those?" she asked, her gaze on David. He looked calm and dangerous. She hoped, prayed, he wouldn't try anything. His eyes moved over her with an urgency that told her he'd do what he had to do—to save her.

She could hear the discussion over the radio. "We have a visual, Godwin. Keep 'em talking."

"What do you want?" she asked the man, her eyes moving over him, taking in details. She spotted the tattoo right away. Just as David had described it and exactly like the one she'd seen, too.

Her heart jumped and skidded, making her feel lightheaded. Whitney blinked and took a deep breath. She had to stay calm and in control. But her mind was screaming, *Why David? Why did he somehow always show up at the worst possible time?*

Maybe there would never be a good time for them. He was used to rescuing people in danger. And that meant her, too.

She wanted him in her life, but not like this. Not ever like this.

The man chuckled and yanked David back against him. "First, I want you to call off the marksman who's got his rifle trained on me. If he shoots me, your friend here goes with me."

Whitney closed her eyes to that image. "How can you be so sure?" she asked, certain that team member and former soldier Tristan McKeller had a high-powered rifle trained on them right now. The chief would do everything he could to save David, but if he ordered Tristan to take the shot…it could go wrong. So wrong.

"We can talk," she said. "Give us a name, and you might be able to get off easier. Who's in charge?"

"I'm not making any deals," the man said. He glanced back behind him.

"Is your friend out there?" Whitney asked, holding the man and David in her gaze. "Is he the other shooter?"

"What do you think?" the man asked. "We want what we left on the train, lady. And we need you to bring it to us."

"You mean the drugs. The duffels full of heroin? You sure didn't hide that very well. Your boss must be fuming by now."

Again, he looked over his shoulder. Was he running scared or running out of options?

"Tell your people to bring the bags. Then, nobody gets hurt."

"You want us dead, right?" David said. "Kind of stupid. Now everyone knows who you are."

"We should have killed both of you the first time," the man shouted.

"If she goes, I go with her," David said, his eyes on Whitney.

She at least agreed with that. She wouldn't let them take him.

"Shut up!" The man yanked at David again, but this time David shoved back, a full-on slam with his entire body.

Whitney gasped as the man hit David on the side of the head with the butt of the gun, but it gave her one quick instant to do what she had to do.

Taking a glance down the track, she called out to Hunter. "Attack!" Then she looked into David's eyes, saw the blood running down his cheek and screamed, "Get down, David."

David stepped back, knocking the man away with a grunt as he elbowed his attacker and then fell to the ground and rolled away. The man screamed his rage, lifted on one knee and turned with the gun toward David. But Hunter was already running, leaping, barking in a snarling frenzy.

Whitney cringed, her gun lifted, a silent scream trapped inside her throat. She called out, "Drop the weapon."

The man kept turning toward where David lay, but David rolled and grabbed at the man's leg, bringing him off balance as he fired. The shot hit the rocks as David brought him down.

Then Hunter leaped into the air, his teeth exposed, and bit into the man's bare arm. The suspect screamed and writhed, but Whitney didn't call off her partner.

"Hold," she told Hunter.

"Suspect subdued," Whitney said into the radio, running, her gun still drawn. When she heard shots firing all around them, she didn't care.

She was headed straight for David.

"I'm okay."

David kept telling Whitney that, but she didn't seem to believe him. He was sitting in the back of an ambulance, but he didn't plan on going to the hospital.

Another ambulance had already taken Eddie away, but not before Whitney had run up to the big man and gave him a hug. "Eddie, you're my hero," she'd told the embarrassed-looking officer.

"I might be your hero, Godwin," Eddie had replied on a hoarse chuckle. "But…I am definitely retiring at the end of this year. I've had enough."

Now Whitney stared at David, her blue eyes alert in spite of the lines of fatigue etched around them. "I still can't believe you did that," she said, anger warring with admiration in her tone. "What were you thinking?"

"I didn't know what else to do," he said, memories of getting reamed out by her and the chief and several other officers still burning through his brain. "I followed the blue car here, and then I heard shooting."

"You could have been killed," she said, her tone low and quiet. "How many times do I have to explain this to you?"

"I'm here and I'm fine," he replied. "I was a distraction, so it all worked out."

"This time," she said, her blue eyes holding him and making him want to tug her close and hold on to her forever.

But David couldn't do that. Not now. Not today.

He didn't tell her why he'd been in the train station, and in all the excitement of arresting the man who'd held David, she hadn't asked. Yet.

"Well, yes, it did work out. The DEA has carted away the suspect and the drugs. No one was killed, thankfully, and the train is back on track, so to speak."

"But the other one got away," David said, wishing he could have exposed both of them. "When Tattoo Man showed up and held me, I'd already decided I wasn't falling for his tricks. I would have taken him."

"I don't like your recklessness and bravery," Whitney retorted. "Your man, better known as Ramon Catez, is with the DEA now. If he talks, we might get somewhere." She shook her head. "But…he seemed really scared. I don't think he'll talk at all. He knows the consequences if he does."

David wanted to pull her close and kiss her. But with so many people walking around, including that pesky reporter Madison Coles from the *Canyon County Gazette*, he didn't dare make a move.

"Can I go now?" he asked, knowing he'd have to tell Whitney he'd decided to leave Desert Valley. Or maybe he'd leave without any more words. That might be the best way to handle this.

"You should be checked out."

"I'm fine. Just a black eye." He winced when he touched the spot on his temple where Catez had slammed him with the handgun.

"I'm sorry about our dinner," she replied. When she heard the chief calling her name, she said, "I have to go. I'll call you later."

"Better yet, come by the Rose," he said, wanting to hold her one more time even if he didn't have the guts to tell her the truth. "Miss Rosa is saving dinner for us."

"I'm starving," she said. "Maybe I'll do that." Then, after a quick glance, she touched her hand to his wound. "Thank you, David."

While he appreciated her gratitude and her

attitude, David wanted more. He signed off on not going to the ER and got back in Miss Rosa's yellow truck without buying a train ticket.

But he was going to have to leave, and soon. He just didn't know how to say goodbye.

David sent Miss Rosa to bed, promising her he'd heat up the dinner she'd prepared. But he didn't have an appetite.

So here he sat, staring out into the late-night moonlight, wondering how he was going to get back on that train and leave Whitney.

What else could he do?

He had fallen for her in a fast and easy way that scared him. Was he reacting to everything they'd been through? Or did he really love her? Lucas had talked about her so much and David had carried that picture of her for so long, he felt as if he'd always known her. And yet he wanted to know more.

He'd been here only a couple of weeks. It didn't make any sense. Was he projecting all the pain and sorrow he'd experienced, including the death of her brother, onto her, expecting her to fix all of his problems?

Or had Lucas sent him here for this very thing—hoping that he and Whitney would fall in love?

Help me, Lord. Help me to see what I need to do next. He prayed about his past life, asking God to release him from this tremendous guilt that pulled at him like quicksand. He prayed for his future, wishing he could find some hope.

David felt as if he were traipsing around in a vast wilderness, searching for something. Searching for someone.

He closed his eyes, thinking he'd never felt so lonely in his life.

And then he heard a gentle knock at the door.

Getting up, he walked through the dark hallway of the big house. The other guests had gone to bed long ago, so the old house was quiet now, its Victorian sofas and velvet curtains hushed in a muted gray wash of color. David looked through the side window by the stained-glass front door and saw Whitney standing there.

She'd come.

He opened the door with a smile and a bittersweet heart. "Hi."

"Hi. Am I too late?"

He didn't know how to answer that, so he did what he should have done sooner. He pulled her inside, shut the door and kissed her. Then he whispered, "No. You're right on time."

The food was amazing.

Whitney bit into another strawberry, her mind

on that kiss instead of her full stomach. She'd eaten out of nervousness and relief. Her nerves were frazzled and frayed, but she'd learned something in today's standoff.

She was a survivor. And she so wanted to be the best police officer she could possibly be. She'd also realized that she'd been holding back in all the other areas of her life because she was afraid to take a chance again.

Lucas knew her so well. She could imagine her brother handpicking the perfect man for her.

And that man had trekked across the world to show her what Lucas had seen all along. That she needed someone solid and good in her life.

She was falling for the medic.

But…now that she'd come to that conclusion, something wasn't right. David's actions tonight were subdued and quiet. Not his usual good-natured teasing and flirting.

She stared over at him. "You're tired. I should go."

"No, don't." He got up, came around the table and pulled her up. "You look so pretty."

She grinned and touched a hand to her hair. "I changed in a hurry. Gina and Ellen insisted I needed to come see you."

"Ah, so I have Gina and Ellen to thank for this midnight supper."

"Yes. Shelby was asleep and Hunter was

tired, so they both insisted on staying so I could see you. Told me to put on a dress and some lipstick and get over here."

"I like your friends." He touched a finger to Whitney's nose. "And I like this dress."

Whitney giggled at that, thinking she felt young and carefree in the blue maxidress in spite of being exhausted. But David made her feel alive in a way that no one else ever had.

She reached up a hand to his face, touching his swollen eye. "I was so scared today when I saw that man holding a gun on you."

He put his hand over hers. "You were as cool as anyone I've ever seen. You handled the situation."

"My heart was about to come out of my chest," she replied, shaking her head. "I need to explain to you again, David. You don't have to protect me."

He pulled away, and she realized this was the *something* between them. It wasn't in his nature to ignore someone in danger. He'd been trained to help people who were in danger or injured, to minister to them and keep them alive. How could she ask him to give up the very essence of his being? They'd clash at every turn.

"I know you can take care of yourself," he finally said. "But I'm still having some flashbacks about...seeing people die while in battle."

"So you have to step in. You haven't learned how to tamp that down yet."

"No, I haven't."

He turned to her, his eyes dark in the moonlight. "Old habits die hard."

"But this isn't a habit for you, David. This is what you're trained to do."

"Yes. I need to refocus that training on medicine. In a hospital. In the clinic, anywhere except…when I'm near you."

She moved toward him, hoping to make him see what she felt in her heart. "Lucas did this. It's his fault. He sent you here as a proxy for all his worries. He was my big brother, my protector, but he hovered and worried. I needed to breathe. I had to find my own way. And I did, in spite of everything."

"Yeah, and you're not ready to give up your independence. I don't expect you to do that. Not for me."

"So where does that leave us?" she asked. "Can't we try? Once this is all over, I could be moving on anyway."

"Is that what you want?"

"I want a lot of things, but I have a job that I love, and I want to be the best at it. I also want a life away from work. I want to be a good mother to Shelby. I'm still struggling to find that balance."

"And I'm still struggling to find my footing back on solid ground. It's a long process."

"Should I go?" she asked, wanting to stay.

He looked into her eyes, a war exploding in his dark gaze. Then he pulled her into his arms. "No, don't go. Not yet."

He kissed her again, the moonlight washing over them in shades of pale gray and shimmering blue. Whitney gave in to the thousands of emotions flowing through her. Fear, heat, need, want, hope and despair, faith that this could work, doubt that they'd ever make it. She was willing to make it work, willing to give him time, willing to do whatever it would take to make it right this time. With this man.

The right man for her.

They moved over to the white wicker love seat and sat together, touching, holding on, whispering. They talked about their best dreams and their worst fears.

"Do you think Lucas would approve of us being together?" he asked, his hand holding hers.

"I'd like to think that," she admitted. "If not, then why did he make you promise to come here and find me?"

"He worried about you."

"Yes, but he had to know you wouldn't walk away once you got here."

"What if I can't live up to what he expected of me, of what you might expect from me?"

"I don't expect anything," she said. "I want someone in my life who I can trust and enjoy being around."

"Do I fit that bill?"

She kissed him to show him that he fit perfectly. But in her heart, she felt him pulling away. Had today been the last straw for him?

"I have to get home," she finally said, wishing she could do more to ease his pain. "Tomorrow, I write up more reports and keep looking for that other suspect and his boss."

"And what about Brian?"

That question threw her. "I'll keep investigating the house fire and hope I can come up with a clue or connection that can give us a break."

"What if you never find the answers?"

So this was between them, too.

"I have to find the answers."

"But…what if you can't? Are you willing to live with that?"

She'd never thought beyond finding the truth. Was she willing to let it go and get on with her life? "I don't know," she said, trying to be honest. "Can *you* live with *that*?"

"I don't know," he said. Then he added, "But it's not about me. I didn't know Brian. It's about you and your feelings for him."

David wanted her to let go of those feelings. Could she?

She left him standing on the front porch. She was more confused than ever but also more sure than ever.

She wanted David in her life. Now she'd have to hope he'd want to stay in her life.

Whitney went home and lay in her bed, asking God to guide her on all of these conflicting, life-changing decisions.

Back at the Rose, David stared out into the moonlight, his heart heavy with the sure knowledge that he'd kissed the woman he loved for the first and probably the last time.

NINETEEN

Monday, David went to the clinic, intent on telling Dr. Pennington that he was done. He'd tried to find evidence of any wrongdoing on the doctor's part, but so far, he couldn't pin anything on Pennington.

The man did his job, and the patients seemed to keep coming back in spite of his brusque manner. After carefully watching Pennington, David couldn't say for sure if he was using any kind of drugs himself. No erratic behavior, no dilated pupils, no signs of wear and tear or needle marks. But he could be involved in selling illegal drugs on the side. The man drove a nice sports car and lived in a fancy house on a swanky canyon road.

He also apparently had friends in high places, since he bragged about having dinner with politicians and business leaders around the area.

Whatever was going on with the doctor,

David didn't need this kind of disruption in his life.

But when David had walked into the clinic three hours earlier, the place had been in chaos. He'd dived right in, handling an elderly woman who had developed pneumonia and a toddler with an allergic reaction to a bee sting. Then he'd examined patient after patient, which had kept him hopping until late in the day.

"You should get paid," one of the weary nurses told him as she was heading out the door. "Better yet, you should apply to practice medicine here permanently and take over this clinic."

David could see himself doing that, but he had to stick to his plan. He couldn't stay around and watch Whitney while she still carried a torch for another man. And he certainly couldn't deal with the dangers she faced every day. He knew if he remained here, these issues would push them apart.

And yet, he wanted to stay. He had sensed that she wanted the same but…how could they make it happen?

Maybe if he stepped away and gave her some time, they could try again when things settled down. That would give him time to accept her line of work, too.

David went about his business, clearing away supplies and sterilizing instruments. By the time he was done, Dr. Pennington had left. Deciding he'd write a note and leave it on the doctor's door, David did one last check of all the clinic rooms and then headed down the hallway to the doctor's office.

Whitney was glad this Monday was over.

She'd been questioned over and over by the chief and several DEA agents about her handling of the train incident. Not because she'd done anything wrong, as the chief pointed out. But because she had to explain why David Evans had gotten caught up in the middle of things yet again.

"He saw the blue Camaro that followed him and that we know was seen near the Desert Rose Inn," she'd told the chief.

"So he followed the car to the train station? Why was David headed that way?"

Good question. She didn't have an answer, and she hadn't thought to ask David. She'd just been glad he was safe and that they'd had a wonderful couple of hours together.

The man they'd arrested wasn't talking, however. Ramon Catez had a long rap sheet and was known to hang with alleged drug dealers and unscrupulous characters. But he refused to give up the goods on whoever his boss was.

He'd rather rot in prison than face the person in control, apparently.

The lab had found DNA on the red cap and the torn pants fabric. The torn fabric from a pants leg connected Catez to the first drug run, and the red hat they'd found at the Rose had been matched to his partner through the DNA found on both. But the other man was on the run and was now wanted for questioning. They still didn't know who was running the whole show. The man she'd shot had been identified, but he was a petty criminal—a junkie they couldn't connect to anyone.

Now, with that question of why David was at the train station burning inside her head, Whitney headed home with Hunter in the back of the old squad car. She hadn't seen David or heard from him since Friday night. She'd purposely given him time to think about what was happening between them.

And herself time to absorb being with him. Still amazed that she'd fallen for him, Whitney cautioned herself to take things slow. If David decided to stick around, they didn't have to rush anything.

She'd turned onto Desert Valley Road when she noticed a red car parked near a rutted side road up ahead. The vehicle didn't look familiar, but it caused all of her instincts to kick into overdrive. When a scrawny teenager got out of the car and waved her down, Whitney pulled over but left Hunter in the patrol car.

"What the problem?" she asked, taking in the teen's demeanor. "Did your car break down?"

"Yes." He nodded. "It's out of gas. But someone went to get some for me." He shrugged. "I got kind of scared, waiting here by myself. Glad you came along."

Whitney glanced around. "Okay. I can wait with you."

He nodded, his dark eyes darting here and there.

Then Whitney noticed something familiar about the young man. He had the three-feathers tattoo on his left arm.

Drawing her weapon, she said, "You need to show me some ID."

The boy's frightened eyes widened. "They made me do it," he said on a shattered breath. "I'm sorry, lady."

Then she heard another vehicle approaching from the rutted road into the woods. A black SUV, coming right at her.

"Get out of here now," she shouted to the boy, her weapon drawn. Then she hurried back to her own car, but not before the ping of bullets hit the ground around her.

The boy took off running into the woods. Whitney radioed for backup and gave the boy's description while she retreated from the approaching SUV.

She skidded onto the main road and started toward the police station. She looked up to see a silver sports car passing by, and she glanced over and into the startling blue eyes of Dr. William Pennington.

Still shocked by his hostile glare, she watched in her rearview mirror to see where the doctor was headed. He kept going on into town.

Did she follow him or try to get away from the SUV?

She rounded a curve about two miles away from the station and looked in the rearview as the SUV suddenly came up on her tail.

Grabbing the mic to the radio, she reported in. "Suspicious vehicle tailing me. Headed back your way. Send patrol."

Then she checked the rearview again.

And saw a man with a gun hanging out the passenger-side window. He fired a shot as she rounded the curve. She heard the spray of bullets pelting off the back of the car. Hunter started barking.

"Down," she screamed, hoping to keep her partner from being shot.

They'd thought they were through with the drug traffickers.

But they were back.

Whitney knew they'd kill her this time.

And they'd go after David, too.

She had to warn him to be careful with Dr. Pennington.

Because from the look she'd seen in the doctor's eyes and with this SUV chasing her, she knew without a doubt that the doctor had to be the mysterious drug boss who'd been playing all of them.

David hurried into the swank office, notepad in hand. But he couldn't find a pen. When he didn't see one on Dr. Pennington's desk, he opened a drawer. Nothing there except prescription pads. Where did the doctor keep all of his expensive gold pens?

Turning to the bookcase and credenza, he searched for something to write with, his thoughts on what he should say.

Sorry, I'm done. Best wishes.

Sorry, Dr. Pennington, but I have to leave Desert Valley.

What could he say?

That he'd fallen for the one woman he couldn't have? That Whitney's brother had asked him to check on her, he'd gone above and beyond that duty and he never wanted to leave her?

That he suspected everyone around him of being involved in drug trafficking and a conspiracy and murder? And that he couldn't stand by and watch Whitney put her life on the line the same way he'd seen her brother do?

He dug through a narrow drawer on the credenza, his fingers grasping for a pen. At about the time his hand hit on something, his phone buzzed against the pocket of his jeans. Ignoring the phone for now, he felt around again.

A small object.

David tugged at the drawer, but the object had jammed against the top of the bookcase. Slipping his hand inside, he managed to lift it out of the way so he could open the drawer wider. When he had the drawer all the way out, he stopped and took in a breath.

A small plaque of some kind or maybe even a paperweight. Black with gold etchings. An arrow pointed upward, three feathers dangling below its tip.

The three feathers.

Why hadn't he seen this before?

The doctor had obviously hidden it way back in this drawer a long time ago, and since he didn't like people walking into his office, he must have thought no one would ever find it.

And yet, he never locked the office door.

Absentminded or too confident for his own good?

None of that mattered now. David had to get this to the police.

He lifted the square plaque with the tail of his shirt and started toward the supply room to find a paper envelope, and maybe a pen, too. When he got there, he stopped. The door was shut. He hadn't locked it up yet, and he didn't remember closing the door earlier when he'd grabbed the notepad from in here.

David glanced around, the hair on the back of his neck sending a definite warning that he wasn't alone.

He had two choices. He could run as fast as he could toward either door, but he'd already locked the front door. He could make it down the hall to the back but…someone could be out there waiting.

Deciding he'd faced down worse, he didn't choose either of those options. Instead, he opened the supply closet door and barreled inside, hoping he'd knock over whoever must be waiting there. It was his only chance of making it out of here alive.

It worked.

He surprised the man lurking against the door, knocking him down while David landed on top of him, the heavy black glass plaque slipping out of his hand to hit the floor with a heavy thud.

They rolled. David pinned the man down, then stared into his eyes. "You were on the train that day," he shouted, recognizing the shorter, chunky man who'd been wearing the red baseball cap. The man the police had been trying to find.

"Shoulda killed you then," the man spat, struggling to flip David over.

But David held him down, sheer adrenaline giving him the strength he needed to end this. The man eyed him, then glanced over at the plaque. Seeing his intent, David lifted one hand and stretched it toward the sparkling black glass.

While the man he was trying to hold did the same thing.

David had his hand on the heavy, squared-off glass, grunting as he gathered it into his grip. Lifting it, he stared into the eyes of a man he'd never forget.

But before he could bring it down on the attacker's head, a voice behind him halted his hand in midair.

"Don't do it, Evans," Dr. Pennington said in a gruff shout. "I'll kill you myself. And right about now I have someone taking care of that annoying K9 officer, too."

* * *

Whitney heard the shot and then felt a thud right before her car started skidding out of control. They'd hit a tire!

She held tight to the wheel, letting the car do a spin so she wouldn't run off into a ditch on the other side of the road. If she stopped, they'd shoot her on the spot.

"Hunter, hang on," she called to the barking, snarling dog. "Hang on."

She righted the car, faced the SUV head-on and then checked her weapon while holding the steering wheel with one hand. Help was on the way, but she'd have to hold these guys off until someone showed up.

She'd tried to call David to warn him to get out of the clinic. He shouldn't go back to the Desert Rose, either. Too dangerous. But he hadn't answered.

Praying she wasn't too late, Whitney ducked as another round of bullets pierced the glass in front of her. Diving down in the seat, she prayed for her life.

And for backup.

The dark SUV hovered on the road a few yards away. Whitney peeked again to make sure no one was sneaking up on her. When she heard a car door opening, she watched as a tall man dressed in black started toward her, his gun raised.

She didn't have time or a way to let Hunter out to attack the man. And she didn't have time to do anything to protect herself. Except hold on to her gun and shoot for all she was worth.

She hit the button on the driver's-side window to let it down enough that she could shoot out of it. Then she waited for the man to come closer, her breath steady and sure even if her pulse was jumping like a live wire. She thought of Shelby and how much she loved her little girl. She thought of her work, how far she'd come and how Hunter trusted her and kept her safe. And then she thought of David, a man who'd walked into her life out of the blue and captured her heart immediately.

Thank you, Lucas.

She had too much to live for to die here on this dry stretch of road.

"Drop the weapon," she said to the approaching man.

His chuckle hit the silent woods.

When she saw his shadow cast over the still car, she lifted and started shooting through the open window. And she didn't stop until her weapon was empty and she heard sirens approaching.

* * *

David let go of the heavy object in his hand and fell away from the man underneath him. He wasn't surprised to find Dr. Pennington holding a gun on him, but the tremor of fear that shot through him had him glaring up at the man. "You wouldn't hurt Whitney. She's doing her job."

"And her work is interfering with my extra-curricular activities."

David had to be cool. He had to get to Whitney.

"What took you so long? I mean, that was you or some of your underlings who've tried to kill us over and over, right?" he quipped, accepting what he'd seen all along.

He should have acted sooner, taken matters into his own hands. But his focus had been on Whitney and watching over her instead of keeping closer tabs on the man who ran this clinic. Now that one mistake could prove to be fatal. "What do you plan to do?"

Dear God, don't let them hurt her.

"I think you know the answer to that," Dr. Pennington said while his goon got up and yanked David to his feet. "I kept you close to watch you, Evans. Even showing you what can happen when someone disobeys me. But you had to be the noble medic, home from the horror of war. And I had to be careful. Didn't want this to happen here, but…I'm all out of options. People who always do the right thing really get on my nerves."

David took in the situation. No way out of here unless he fought his way out, but then he'd get shot, and that wouldn't help Whitney. But he sure didn't plan on going for a ride with these two, either. They'd fight it out here and end it here, one way or another.

And he had to trust God and trust Whitney. *See us through. See us through.*

If he made it out of here, he'd tell Whitney he never wanted to leave her again.

"I can see how that might annoy you," David replied, his gaze flickering to the strange piece of glass he'd stumbled upon, which now lay forgotten on the floor. "So…did you kill Veronica Earnshaw?"

Dr. Pennington looked surprised, his expression turning to mock hurt. "Do I look like a killer?"

"You look like a lot of things to me," David said. "I wouldn't put it past you."

The doctor shook his head. "I need to vet my volunteers better from now on. You're way too nosy for your own good, Evans."

"I like answers," David retorted. "And the truth."

"I didn't kill Veronica. I loved her." Dr. Pennington's gaze went to a faraway place, hollow and distant. "She used me, of course. Ran around on me, taunted me, made me feel like less than a man. I got angry at her but…I didn't kill her."

David saw a glimmer of redemption in those cold blue eyes. "Then, why do you want to kill Whitney and leave her baby without a mother?"

"Shut up," Dr. Pennington shouted. "You both saw too much. Someone had to have sent you here. DEA? The locals? Who?"

David shook his head. "Are you serious? I only came here to see Whitney since I knew her brother. We served together in Afghanistan. And…I wanted to help out here to stay busy. That's it."

"You saw my men," the doctor shouted. "You're messing where you don't belong."

"We saw two criminals doing what they do best," David said, pushing backward while he talked. "Killing us will only bring the whole police department down on your head. No one sent me, but you were kind of obvious, so this won't end here."

Dr. Pennington started pacing. When he whirled around, he noticed David's foot by the shimmering black plaque. Reaching down, he yanked it up and held it in David's face. "Where did you find this?"

"In your office," David replied. "It reminded me of Ramon Catez's tattoo." He glanced at the man beside him. "I'm guessing he has one, too. Do you make all of your couriers get this tattoo as a symbol of their loyalty? That young boy you were stitching up, did he fail one of your tests?"

"You have no idea how hard I work," the doctor said in reply. "Veronica was a demanding woman, even after she left me."

"So this is her fault?"

"The Three Feathers used to mean something to me," Dr. Pennington said. "I have that tattoo on my back. I've helped a lot of the indigenous people around here. I received this plaque because of my work."

"What happened to you?" David asked.

Pennington shook his head. "I don't know. Power. Money. I needed more. I found a way to get it and to give others a means for a better life."

David felt sorry for the doctor, but he wasn't going to forgive him. "Stop this, Doc. Do whatever to me, but don't kill Whitney."

Dr. Pennington's smile twisted in anger. "It's too late, Evans. She's probably already dead."

David couldn't believe that. He wouldn't believe it.

He looked around and decided he'd get out of

here and get to Whitney. And this time he didn't care who thought he should stay out of her way.

He whirled and shoved the shorter man into a rack full of supplies and then ducked and head butted the doctor, slamming him down. The doctor dropped his prize possession and groaned, but David caught it up and rammed it into Pennington's skull. Then he flipped around, grabbed the gun, turned just as the other man started after him again. David shot the man in the leg.

The doctor moaned and tried to get up. David fisted him in the face and knocked him back down. Then he called 911 and reported what had happened.

"Somebody needs to come and collect these two," he said. "And…you need to find Officer Whitney Godwin and make sure she's okay."

David turned, only to find Dr. Pennington rising up like a ghostly phoenix, a pair of scissors in his hand. He rushed at David, a dark madness in his steel-cold eyes.

David backed up as the back door burst open and Whitney ran toward him, with officers and K9s on her heels.

"Bite!"

Hunter did his job. The big dog leaped into the air, landed solidly against the startled doctor and knocked him to the floor. Then Hunter sank his teeth into the doctor's arm. Dr. Pennington screamed and dropped the scissors as they went down. Hunter held him there on the floor.

Whitney rushed up the hallway.

"David," she shouted. "David, are you okay?"

"I am now," David said, grabbing her close.

All this time, he'd been the one anxious to save Whitney, but she'd been the one who'd saved him. By letting him into her life and her heart.

"I'm fine now," he said as he took her into his arms.

He'd never let her go again.

TWENTY

Two days later, Chief Jones stood staring out at the whole department. Whitney sat with Hunter curled at her feet, her fellow rookies gathered with their own partners at their sides, too. She'd been cleared for duty yet again after the incident out on the road, but she had one more afternoon of free time after this meeting. That free time had been ordered by the chief.

She'd wounded the man who'd tried to kill her out on the road.

He was still at the medical center, being heavily guarded. And based on the DNA evidence they'd gotten back from the Flagstaff lab, they'd managed to confirm that the red cap belonged to the man who'd attacked David in the clinic, which could prove he was the other man who'd been involved in the train smugglings. They'd also found the young man who'd been with the stalled car—the same teen David had helped stitch up—hiding in the woods, afraid, hungry and covered with bug bites. He'd signed on with Dr. Pennington's drug ring to earn money for his impoverished family, but soon he'd found out the doctor would never let him leave. Whitney had made sure he got the help he needed from the proper authorities to hopefully turn his life around.

She'd had help with her life from the local church, so she knew this boy could be saved from a life of drugs and crime.

Chief Jones gave her one of his rare smiles. "Let's give Officer Whitney Godwin a big hand for nabbing a local drug dealer and busting up his ring."

Everyone clapped, and even stoic Ryder Hayes gave her a nod and a smile. Wishing she could find out who'd murdered his wife, Whitney vowed to keep working toward that goal. But she had to decide what she was going to do about her need to find Brian's killer. She didn't want that to come between David and her.

While the chief went over the details of Dr. Pennington's elaborate drug activities and assured them that the doctor would be tried and put away for his crimes, Whitney's thoughts went back to David.

"I can't leave you," he'd whispered to her when she'd found him at the clinic.

Had he been planning on doing that? It didn't

take much police work to figure out he'd been headed toward the train station because he was planning to buy a ticket. So later that night, when he'd come to her house and held her close, she'd asked him outright.

"But you were going to leave me, right?"

He'd nodded. "Yes, and then I saw the blue car and followed it. Even after all of that, I still thought leaving would be the best thing for you. And maybe for me, since I wasn't handling things very well. I thought if I stayed I'd be in the way. Hindering you at every turn is not a good way to begin a relationship. And in this case, it was kind of dangerous, too."

"No, not exactly good but…you are my hero, no matter what."

"Do you want me to stay, then?"

"Do you think you can learn to live with me being a K9 officer?"

He'd stared down at her, his hands touching her hair, his eyes full of an endearing fear mixed with a dollop of hope. "I don't think I have any other choice, Whitney. I love you."

"I love you, too," she'd told him, tears in her eyes, joy in her heart. "But…are we rushing this? Should we step back and see how we do?"

"We've been through the worst," he'd said. "It can only get better from here."

She wanted better.

Whitney loved him. This feeling far out-weighed the feelings she'd had for Brian. Brian had been good-looking and charming but…she could see now what she'd denied before. All of the signs had been there, in the way he flirted with everyone from Carrie to Gina and Sophie and even Veronica. In the way he'd always demanded they stay in at his house rather than taking her out on real dates and showing her the hundreds of different ways he could love her.

And he'd done the flirting right in front of Whitney. He'd chosen her over the others because she'd been the one to cave.

She didn't want to cave. She wanted to love. Really love a man who'd done nothing but try to protect her. A man who shared her values and who believed in faith and hope and love even though he'd been through war and disaster and death.

If she let David go, she might lose the best man for her. The one man who could match her and allow her to be his equal. Her soul mate.

"I don't want you to leave," she'd finally told David. "I don't want you to go."

So he was staying here until this case was solved, and then they'd decide where they'd wind up. "I don't care if we stay here or go to Tucson," he'd told her. "I want to be with you." Then he'd kissed her. "And I'm going to learn to trust you and God when it comes to your line of work."

He also told her he really wanted to take over the Desert Valley Clinic and get it in top shape. "That way, if we leave, it'll be ready for the next doctor."

Whitney couldn't think of a better plan.

And she couldn't wait to spend the afternoon with David.

After Chief Jones had gone over the particulars of the drug case, he moved to the investigation of Veronica's death. "We're hitting roadblocks, but we're not gonna give up. We've canvassed neighborhoods looking for Marco, the missing puppy, and we know someone is breaking into a lot of the homes around the training area. They have to be looking for something. And so are we. Marco. That little puppy might hold the clue to whoever murdered Veronica."

Chief Jones stopped and glanced around. "I also want everyone to be aware about the upcoming Canyon County Police Dance and Fundraiser in May. We've established that for the past two years on the night of the dance, a rookie has died. Both deaths occurred at their homes and right before the dance. I've had some of you investigating these incidents, and these mysterious deaths are a matter of concern for all of us."

He looked at James Harrison, who sat near Whitney. "Especially you, Harrison. You've got the markings—blond hair and good looks. That seems to be the pattern." He winked, but his tone was serious. "I suggest all of you be alert on that day and be careful about being alone. Get dressed with the doors locked and the lights on and your partners on guard."

"I could try to draw out the killer, Chief," James said with a shrug. As if it was no big deal at all.

Whitney breathed a sigh of relief when the chief disagreed with that idea. "Harrison, you're already a target. Don't push your luck. All of you, be aware. We've got enough to deal with, and I don't want to lose another good officer."

After the meeting broke up, James leaned over to Whitney. "I want to do something, but I don't know what else can be done."

"I know what you mean," Whitney said. "I feel the same way." They headed out toward the parking lot. "I'll be watching out for you, Harrison."

"Thanks," James said.

Whitney glanced around and spotted David waiting for her by Miss Rosa's bright yellow truck. Hunter's ears perked up.

"Let's go," she said to Hunter, her smile meant for David.

He kissed her hello as the others filed out.

Whitney didn't care what the others saw now. She was done with secrets and hiding. She planned to tell her friends the truth about Brian being Shelby's father. But right now she only wanted to spend a nice afternoon with David.

"How'd it go?" he asked, his expression free of the weariness she'd first seen in him. And he looked great in his faded blue T-shirt and old jeans.

"Okay. We haven't made a lot of progress on Veronica's murder, but at least we got a drug ring off the streets."

"You did that," he reminded her with pride.

"You helped," she shot back.

"Right." They both laughed, and he pulled her close. "Wanna get out of here?"

"Yes."

"You two are so cute together," Carrie said as she walked by with a container of leftover cookies she'd brought to roll call. "Whitney, enjoy your last afternoon off before you get back out there."

Whitney nabbed two oatmeal cookies. "I will, Carrie. Thanks." She sure appreciated what a great baker the department secretary was.

David nibbled on his cookie, and then he nibbled at her ear. "How about a long hike along the river?"

"I'd love that."

They got into the old truck, and he turned to kiss her again. "And...later we can pick up Shelby, and I'll make dinner for you."

Words that made her swoon.

Later, as they sat on some boulders near the gurgling water, Whitney turned to David. "I won't quit trying to figure out these deaths, but I want you to know I'm going to back off a little regarding what happened to Brian. I need to work with the team, and I'll talk to the chief about that, too. I can't do it alone, and you can't help me. You have a lot to do while we're still here."

He took her hand in his. "I'll rest easier knowing you're not setting yourself up as a target. I like the team concept."

"I like the you-and-me concept," she said.

He kissed her again. He seemed to like doing that, and she sure liked his kisses. Then his brown eyes went to dark chocolate. "I know we're not supposed to rush this but...one day soon...I'm going to ask you to marry me."

Whitney's heart was already rushing. "You are?"

"Yes, and after that I'm going to go about adopting Shelby so...so that...I can be her father. If that's okay with you, I mean?"

Whitney wasn't a crier. She never cried.

She hated crying and she pushed tears away. Far away.

But now she couldn't hold them back. Tears poured down her face, and all the angst and fear and despair she'd held back for the past year came tumbling down in a flood of emotion, only to be replaced with a flood of joy. She'd lost everything…but here in David's arms, she'd found herself.

"Do you want that?" he asked, his fingers catching her tears.

"I do," she said, bobbing her head. "I do want that."

"Okay, then," he replied, his hands moving over her face. "Okay. We'll make it happen, and when I ask you, we'll have dinner at the Rose, and Miss Rosa will make us something decadent and I'll get down on one knee—"

"And I'll say yes. I'll say yes, David."

"Sounds like a plan."

They sat and talked about the future while the sun turned the desert and woods shades of pink and burned orange. Then they held each other and watched the sun set over the river—with the promise of rising again tomorrow.

* * * * *

If you liked this ROOKIE K-9 UNIT *novel,*
watch for the next book in the series,
SEEK AND FIND by Dana Mentink.

Dear Reader,

David and Whitney proved to be two very determined and stubborn characters. They were both brave and noble, but they were afraid to let go of control enough to figure out how to make their relationship work. When two strong personalities fall in love, things can get a bit intense. The challenge came in trying to get past the danger in their lives so they could find their happily-ever-after.

This story brought out a lot of questions. How do you honor a promise made in the heat of battle? How do you try to protect someone who doesn't want your protection? How do you prove your love when you're too afraid to love again?

In the end, David had to realize that Whitney was strong enough to match him and to save him.

I think we sometimes fight God's love in the same way. We think we can take care of things when really we don't have a lot of control over every aspect of our lives. We have to trust in His love.

I hope you enjoyed this story and I know you'll enjoy the entire Rookie K-9 Unit series.

I am honored to write along with these fabulous authors!

Until next time, may the angels watch over you. Always. ☺

Lenora Worth

LARGER-PRINT BOOKS!

GET 2 FREE
LARGER-PRINT NOVELS
PLUS 2 FREE
MYSTERY GIFTS

Love Inspired®

Larger-print novels are now available...

YES! Please send me 2 FREE LARGER-PRINT Love Inspired® novels and my 2 FREE mystery gifts (gifts are worth about $10). After receiving them, if I don't wish to receive any more books, I can return the shipping statement marked "cancel." If I don't cancel, I will receive 6 brand-new novels every month and be billed just $5.49 per book in the U.S. or $5.99 per book in Canada. That's a savings of at least 19% off the cover price. It's quite a bargain! Shipping and handling is just 50¢ per book in the U.S. and 75¢ per book in Canada.* I understand that accepting the 2 free books and gifts places me under no obligation to buy anything. I can always return a shipment and cancel at any time. Even if I never buy another book, the two free books and gifts are mine to keep forever.

122/322 IDN GH6D

Name _____ (PLEASE PRINT)

Address _____ Apt. #

City _____ State/Prov. _____ Zip/Postal Code

Signature (if under 18, a parent or guardian must sign)

Mail to the **Reader Service**:
IN U.S.A.: P.O. Box 1867, Buffalo, NY 14240-1867
IN CANADA: P.O. Box 609, Fort Erie, Ontario L2A 5X3

**Are you a current subscriber to Love Inspired® books
and want to receive the larger-print edition?
Call 1-800-873-8635 or visit www.ReaderService.com.**

* Terms and prices subject to change without notice. Prices do not include applicable taxes. Sales tax applicable in N.Y. Canadian residents will be charged applicable taxes. Offer not valid in Quebec. This offer is limited to one order per household. Not valid to current subscribers to Love Inspired Larger-Print books. All orders subject to credit approval. Credit or debit balances in a customer's account(s) may be offset by any other outstanding balance owed by or to the customer. Please allow 4 to 6 weeks for delivery. Offer available while quantities last.

Your Privacy—The Reader Service is committed to protecting your privacy. Our Privacy Policy is available online at www.ReaderService.com or upon request from the Reader Service.

We make a portion of our mailing list available to reputable third parties that offer products we believe may interest you. If you prefer that we not exchange your name with third parties, or if you wish to clarify or modify your communication preferences, please visit us at www.ReaderService.com/consumerchoice or write to us at Reader Service Preference Service, P.O. Box 9062, Buffalo, NY 14240-9062. Include your complete name and address.

LILP15

LARGER-PRINT BOOKS!

GET 2 FREE
LARGER-PRINT NOVELS
PLUS 2 FREE
MYSTERY GIFTS

Love Inspired®

SUSPENSE
RIVETING INSPIRATIONAL ROMANCE

Larger-print novels are now available...

REQUEST YOUR FREE BOOKS!

2 FREE INSPIRATIONAL NOVELS
PLUS 2 *FREE* MYSTERY GIFTS

Love Inspired® HISTORICAL